Dan Fowler
G-Man
Volume Four

Airship 27 Productions

Dan Fowler: G-Man Volume Four

"SkyHook," "In Charge" ©2024 Fred Adams Jr.

Edited by Ron Fortier
Associate Editor: Jonathan Sweet

Cover illustration ©2024 Michael Youngblood
Interior illustrations ©2024 Sam Salas
Production and design by Rob Davis
Marketing management by Michael Vance

Published by
Airship 27 Productions
www.airship27hangar.com

ISBN: 978-1-953589-87-3

Printed in the United States of America

10 9 8 7 6 5 4 3 2 1

Dan Fowler
G-Man
Volume Four

SKYHOOK

The uniformed driver turned to his sidekick. "Any sandwiches left, Lou?" Charlie Foster didn't mind driving the whole run from Denver to Arizona. In fact, he preferred driving the International armored van to riding shotgun like Gabby Hayes in some cowboy serial. The payload was a big one, eighty-two thousand dollars in newly minted Walking Liberty halves headed for delivery to banks in Phoenix.

The weather was good, the traffic was light, and Charlie had driven the same route enough times that he could drive it and read a magazine at the same time, although that would likely get him fired. Plugging along at a steady forty-five, he expected to arrive at their first drop off in three hours. Outside the window, the moonlit desert spread like a grey blanket in every direction when the clouds parted and the Moon, about to dip over the mountains to their right, shone like a pale spotlight, casting long shadows across the sand from the scrub and rocks.

Lou rummaged in the paper sack on his lap. "You got your choice: ham and Swiss, or Swiss and ham. Bill ate the last chicken salad an hour ago." He rapped on the glass divider and the guard in the hopper waved.

"I don't know why we need him along with all the chaperones we have." Charlie pointed to the dark sedan in front of them with three company guards. Behind them, an identical car followed. "Nobody in his right mind would try to knock off this shipment."

"Company rules, Charlie."

Charlie snorted. "And the company rules say forty-five miles per hour. On this straightaway, I could do eighty easy and we'd be there a lot quicker."

Lou unwrapped the waxed paper and handed Charlie the sandwich. As he did, the escort car in front of them exploded in a ball of orange fire. Charlie jammed on the brakes, but the heavy truck had too much momentum to keep it from ramming the flaming wreckage. A boom behind them, and the second car blew up.

A black shadow glided over the van, as if a storm cloud had blotted out the Moon. "What the hell?" Charlie craned his neck to see above them. He didn't dare roll down a window or open a door, let alone stick his head out. Overhead he heard a rumbling noise. Something heavy fell onto the van, rocking it. Charlie grabbed the microphone of the two-way radio and opened the channel. "Code six! Code Six! Tango Romeo one-two-seven!"

The receiver crackled. "What is your…" The speaker howled like a siren as a powerful signal jammed the frequency.

Lou looked in the side mirrors and saw a huge steel claw closing around the truck. Metal screeched as the jaws tightened. "Move! Get us out of here," he shouted. "Push the wreck out of your way."

Charlie jammed the gears and popped the clutch. The van pushed at the blazing mass of twisted metal, tires squealing, and started making some headway. It was almost clear when Charlie felt the rear end lift and the tires spin free. The engine screamed as the driveshaft met no resistance. Charlie shut off the engine. Maybe they could try a run for it when they were on the ground again

"Oh, dear God," he said as he watched the pavement, the burning cars, and the desert slip away below them. His first wish was to escape the steel claw. His second, as the car glided through the air was that the claw not let go. Below them the twin fires on the deserted highway faded as the van rose into the air and sailed toward the black wall of the mountains.

"Blow the horn!" Lou shouted. "Flash the lights! Try to get attention!"

Charlie did as he was told, and within thirty seconds, he heard the sound of boots on the roof. At least two pairs of feet. Lou aimed his revolver at the ceiling of the cab. Charlie grabbed his hand.

"Are you crazy? If they can't shoot in, we can't shoot out. The bullets'll ricochet and you'll kill us both."

"What're they doing up there?" They heard a sharp whine as a heavy drill fired up, grinding into the steel plate of the roof over the cargo compartment, right over Bill's seat. In the dim light, they could see Bill, his face twisted with anxiety staring upward. Through the thick glass, Lou and Charlie saw the bit break through, and withdraw. Then they saw a hose snake through the hole, and a thick white cloud of vapor spray from its nozzle.

Charlie clutched at his throat, his eyes wide with pain and terror. He pitched face down. "Jesus," said Lou.

Footsteps overhead.

The drill broke through the roof of the cab.

There was a smell of almonds.

"And how would you like that, Ma'am?" Dan Fowler said, opening the cash drawer under the teller's window. It was nearly noon, and the lobby was almost empty.

"I'd like it all in five dollar bills, please." The elderly lady on the other side of the teller's cage smiled benignly. "I have four grandchildren, and if you would, please give me nice new ones. I hate to give them old rumpled bills."

"Yes, ma'am." He reached into the drawer and his fingers closed on the butt of his .45 automatic. His eye followed Ted Swayze as the thug walked through the revolving door of the Second National Bank followed by his brothers Sam and Orville. All were wearing raincoats on a sunny July afternoon.

Fowler looked to his partner Larry Kendall, who sat nearby at an assistant manager's desk. Kendall nodded tersely and picked up the phone. He had seen them too. The line was open to two agents inside the vault. The Bureau had gotten a tip that the Swayze Brothers would hit Second National that morning, and the Agents were ready and waiting.

Fowler counted out the fives with his left hand, keeping his right on the pistol. The uniformed guard, agent Seth Burns in disguise, sat on a high stool just inside the door. Fowler could feel a bead of sweat run between his shoulder blades and down his back. Look past them, not at them. "Five, ten, fifteen, twenty. There you are ma'am. Have a nice day."

"Oh, and would you please look up my Christmas Club balance for me?"

"Uh, ma'am, I think you should…"

Sam Swayze swept open his coat and swung a sawed off twelve-gauge Remington pump on a strap, catching the guard full in the face. He went down, and Sam took Burns' revolver from its holster and jammed it in the waistband of his trousers. He fired a shot at the ceiling with the Remington that boomed like a stick of dynamite. "This is a robbery! Nobody moves, nobody gets hurt." His eyes swept the tellers. "No alarms or I shoot everybody I see."

Ted opened his coat and pulled out a shotgun to match his brother's. Orville pulled up a Thompson with a straight clip. Ted vaulted the gated divider and nearly fell as he landed in front of Kendall's desk. He aimed the gun at Larry and threw a canvas sack onto it. "You. Fill it up from the drawers, then we're going into the vault."

Larry took the sack in his right hand and held his left one in the air palm forward. "Okay, Mister. I'll do what you say. Just please don't hurt anybody."

He moved toward the teller windows. Fowler was trying to watch all three of the Swayzes at the same time. If he made a wrong move, Ted would blow a hole in Larry and take a few other people with him. Larry began taking the cash from the first drawer, and Fowler got an idea. He let go of his pistol and covered it with a sheaf of twenties then took a step backward.

Larry got to the second window. Fowler's was next. Over Ted's shoulder, Fowler saw the barrel of an automatic rifle coming out of the vault. *No*, he thought, *not yet*. Wait. Larry was at Fowler's drawer, Ted watching every move. He snarled at Fowler, "Back up, bright eyes." Fowler took two steps back, which put the shotgun out of his reach but put him beside a desk he could use for cover.

Everything happened at once. A customer, a man in a white suit and a straw boater panicked and ran for the door. Sam pulled the trigger, and knocked him off his feet, leaving him lying on the terrazzo floor with red carnations blooming on his chest. The automatic rifle spat a burst at Sam and missed him, whanging off a marble cornice.

Ted's eyes twitched toward the gunshot and Larry swung Fowler's automatic from the drawer and put a round in Ted's shoulder. Fowler rolled behind the desk as Ted's shotgun jerked to the right and blew double-aught buckshot through the spot where Fowler had just been standing. Fowler pulled his back-up piece from an ankle holster. He put two rounds through Ted's forehead before he could fire the shotgun again. Larry swiveled and crouched behind the counter to fire through the grille of the teller's cage.

Orville cut loose with the Thompson, sending a spray of bullets ricocheting off the marble and brass. People screamed, some from terror and some from catching a stray bullet.

Orville leveled a long burst through the open vault door, and one of the agents fell forward into the room. Gunfire answered from inside the vault, and Sam caught one in the shoulder, but he kept firing. Burns grabbed Sam around his knees and tried to pull him down. Sam swung the shotgun toward Burns, and Larry popped up to fire and caught Sam in the neck.

Orville fired another burst, and Larry went down. The remaining agent in the vault cut loose with a burst at Orville, who backed into the revolving door for a getaway. Fowler grabbed Ted's shotgun and dived over the divider, rolling to his feet as he hit and running toward the entrance. His first shot shattered the glass in the door, and he fired as fast as he could ratchet the pump, peppering Orville with buckshot.

Fowler ran to the fallen gunman and kicked the Thompson out of his hands, but it wasn't really necessary. Orville, like his brothers, was dead. Fowler could hear sirens coming up the street. He ran back to the teller cages, where Larry was sitting up, propped against a desk. His shirt was red with blood and pink froth bubbled from a hole in his chest.

Fowler wadded his handkerchief and pressed it against Larry's wound. "Did you get him?"

"Don't try to talk." Fowler loosened Larry's tie. "Yeah, we got all of them."

Uniformed cops were pouring through the jagged glass of the revolving door, stepping on and over Orville's corpse.

Larry let out a wet, ragged cough. "Damn it. Ruined my best suit."

"Shut up and save your breath. The ambulance'll be here soon."

He walked around the divider and saw the little old woman he'd waited on moments before. She was crouched on her hands and knees, head between her elbows. "It's over ma'am. You're safe now."

She raised her head and gave Fowler a glassy-eyed stare. "Wait 'til I tell my grandchildren."

It was mid afternoon when Fowler finally made it back to the Justice Building and his office in the Bureau's D.C. headquarters. He slumped into his chair and pulled a bottle of Old Overholt out of his bottom desk drawer. Dan poured three fingers into a tumbler and was about to drink it when a voice came from the doorway. "I wouldn't drink that just yet. The Director wants to see you. Now."

It was Ellis Stone, an agent who spent more of his time in the Bureau headquarters than the field. Fowler nodded. Stone really didn't have to add "now" to the message. Any summons from the Boss implied an immediate response. He set down his drink and as an afterthought, picked it up again, downed in one draught, and headed for the door.

The Director stood beside his desk, hands clasped behind his back so no one could see him wringing them, as he often did when he was agitated. "Come in Agent Fowler. Shut the door."

Fowler stood beside what the agents jokingly called the Inquisition chairs waiting to be invited to sit. The Director took his time packing his pipe. He scratched a wooden match on the side of the box and let it burn a few seconds before he held it over the bowl. and lighting it. In a moment the scent of Sutliffe's Mixture No. 79 filled the room.

"Do you know why I use a wooden match instead of a lighter, Agent Fowler?"

"No sir."

"Because the chemical flame from the Zippo spoils the taste of the tobacco; the same reason I let the sulfur burn off the match before I light the pipe."

"I see," Fowler said, although he doubted it made any real difference.

Time to get to business. "I heard today was a real Wild West show."

"Yes, sir." Fowler knew better than to attempt any rationalization or defense. "They shot first. Nothing more to say."

"No, sir."

"That's not why I called you in. Whitlock Transport is short one armored van, and the Denver Mint is short eighty-two thousand dollars as of two-thirty this morning."

Fowler shrugged. "Their perfect record couldn't last forever."

The Director glared at him. "The delivery crew are missing too, and six of their company gunmen in escort cars were blown up on the highway."

"Blown up? What was in the van?"

"Eighty-two thousand in silver coin."

Fowler whistled. "That's a nice payday for somebody. Who's on it?"

"The Denver office." He paused. "And you."

Fowler nodded. He was accustomed to being sent places on short notice or none. "How soon do I leave?"

"We have you on a flight to Colorado in two hours. In the meantime, as much information as we have so far is in that file." He pointed at the manila folder with the stem of his pipe.

"What about Treasury? Don't they have a dog in the scrap?"

"As soon as the convoy crossed the border and left Colorado, the crime went interstate. It belongs to us now. They don't like it, but that's not my concern."

"Larry Kendall won't be going along. Who will I take with me?"

"No one. You'll liaison with Pete Cooper, the Denver Bureau Chief."

Fowler nodded. "I worked with him once before when he was in the Miami office. The Reston kidnapping."

"I remember. So does he. That's why he requested you."

"I'll give it my best, sir."

The Director nodded and swiveled his chair to look out the window behind his desk. The meeting was over.

Four hours later, Fowler looked out the window of the twin-engine Airspeed Oxford and saw the Mississippi River below him. The plane and pilot were on loan from the Army Air Corps. He was alone in the passenger section, the other seven seats empty, which suited him fine. He wanted the solitude to study the files without fellow passengers trying to converse or read over his shoulder.

But reading was a chore. The flight was rough, the plane sometimes dropping without warning or bucking in the turbulence. More than once Fowler thought he'd puke in his lap, but he managed to hold onto his lunch. The plane touched down at a civilian airfield in Kansas, little more than a cow pasture with a windsock and an orange and white checkered shed. They quickly refueled and Fowler opted against getting out to stretch his legs for fear he might not climb aboard again.

When he disembarked in Denver, he wanted to punch the pilot in the teeth for rearranging his entrails but reminded himself the guy was just doing his job.

When he climbed down the steps, Pete Cooper was waiting for him, a cigarette dangling from the corner of his mouth. The beefy agent was leaning against a black Ford sedan. His shirtsleeves were rolled to the elbows in the ninety-degree heat, but his fedora still perched over his shock of blond hair. His automatic hung in his shoulder rig as if an afterthought.

"I thought I'd get a break from the heat out here."

"You will when the sun goes down. It'll be about fifty-five overnight. It's the altitude."

"Better than a steamy eighty back in D.C."

"It's a trade off. We're a mile up. There's twenty-five percent less oxygen in the air. No hundred-yard dashes 'til you get used to it."

"I'll try to keep up."

They climbed into the car and drove away, leaving a dust cloud in their wake. "I've read the reports, Coop. What more can you tell me?"

"Not much. A four ton armored van has just vanished. Not a trace."

"Any chance it was rolled onto a flatbed or into a trailer?"

Copper shook his head. "Traffic was restricted on the highway. The Highway Patrol would have known if something big enough to haul the van were on the road."

"How about a truck stashed somewhere nearby?"

"Two feet off the berm on either side, and something that big and heavy would sink to the axles in the sand."

"Sand. Could they have buried the van?"

"Not likely in the fifteen minutes before the Highway Patrol rolled in. You don't bury a full-sized armored van with a couple of number five shovels."

"You might if the hole was dug days before and covered with a canvas tarp. Drive the van into the hole, pull the tarp over it, and throw some sand over it."

"That might work, but there were three planned routes and the one they took was chosen at the last minute by Whitlock's home office. It would take some doing to dig three holes unnoticed and have a crew at each one just in case theirs was on the right road."

"I take it you looked."

Cooper flipped his cigarette butt through the open window. "You bet. On the ground and from the air in a fifty mile radius. No sign. It was as if the van just sprouted wings and flew away."

Fowler was silent for a moment. "Maybe it did."

Volker personally supervised the concealment of the zeppelin in the hollow red rock mesa. Covered with an artful blanket of painted canvas, the airship's hump disappeared from view from the air and was even difficult to spot standing on the mesa's rim. Not that anyone would scale its sheer sides anyway.

His hair was iron grey but he was as strong as any of his crew and pulled the cables alongside the best of them. He was dressed in black trousers and turtle necked sweater that bulged at the shoulders and chest.

The armored van heist was easier than he expected. The take was relatively small considering his expenses, but the coins weren't taken to be spent; he already had more money than he could spend in his lifetime. The shiny new half dollars would serve a different purpose in his scheme. The success of the hijacking was gratifying. If he could snatch an armored car, he could snatch anything that moved on a highway.

Even a limousine.

A mile or so away, his men were emptying the van's cargo. The van would be disposed of and serve as a coffin for the driver and guards.

"Herr Volker." Metz, his second in command, stood at a respectful distance. His disfigured face looked more grotesque in the harsh lamp light than it did in the noonday sun. Volker had selected him for two reasons, one his imposing size and bearing, which commanded respect and obedience from the men, and his unflagging loyalty, not only to the cause, but to Volker himself.

Volker had rescued the soldier of fortune from the penal colony of Cayenne, better known as Devil's Island, along with four of his fellow prisoners, who became the core of his operation. Others he freed from Georgia chain gangs, prisons across the country, and even one from Mississippi's infamous Parchman Farm. Each was given his chance to prove himself and lived or died, accordingly. Those who survived the winnowing would walk into Hell for him without question, and his mission demanded nothing less.

"The coins are transferred from the van. Patterson and Dickey will dispose of it as soon as it's dark."

Volker nodded. "Very good. Has our friend in Whitlock been in touch?"

"Not yet, but he will be. He's an impatient little bastard, and he wants his money."

"Five thousand dollars for the route," Volker said. "He was a fool to embezzle from his employer. He'll never live to pay it back. Mister Pender has become simply a mouth to be silenced."

"He'll collect his due in Hell," Metz said.

Volker cupped his hand around a match to light his cigarette. He inhaled a long pull and let the smoke out before saying, "And so shall we all, Metz. So shall we all."

The drive was a long one to the crime scene, and the agents had plenty of time to hash over the details of the case and float a few theories.

"I even thought the thieves might have quickly repainted the van," Cooper said, "but that wouldn't do any good. Those International Harvester armored vans are shaped like a loaf of pumpernickel. No disguising that."

"I think part of the trouble here was Whitlock Transport's cockiness. They traded for years on their perfect safety record and started believing their own mythology. It was almost like throwing down the glove to criminals, challenging them to just try to rob them."

"I don't know," Cooper said. "Two cars, one in front and one behind the van, each with three armed guards, plus the crew inside. That's not shabby."

"Based on what you've told me, whoever pulled this off was ready for a small army. I doubt the explosives were planted in the cars. They'd need an insider for that."

"I thought of that too. That suggests maybe a bazooka or a mortar."

"Or bombing from the air."

"I could buy an airplane. That would explain the bombed out cars, but taking the whole van? Fowler paused as if hesitating to make the suggestion. "How about a blimp?"

Cooper thought this possibility over for a moment, then nodded and said, "Yeah . . . maybe so. Wouldn't that be a hell of a thing?"

"That's an understatement, Coop."

Cooper pulled to the side of the road where a cluster of Highway Patrol vehicles and unmarked Bureau cars were parked. Off the road, agents were combing the sands to either side, gathering parts of cars and people from the scrub brush and stunted trees.

Two black patches on the pavement marked the explosions, and tire marks showed where the van had tried to stop.

An agent with wire rimmed glasses and sweat rings reaching for each other across his chest saw Cooper and came over. Cooper introduced him as Higgins. "We found the van's front bumper in the wreckage of the lead car," Higgins said. "Looks as if the driver couldn't stop fast enough and rammed it. He left skid marks. Then there are more tracks, peelers this time. Looks as if he spun his wheels trying to push the wreck out of his way. Then they just stop."

Fowler and Coop shared a look and an unspoken thought, and both looked to the sky.

Over steaks and beer in Denver, Fowler and Cooper brainstormed over every detail of the heist.

"But why steal the whole truck?" Cooper said. "Why not just blow the doors with TNT?"

"The getaway opportunities are too limited on the only road through forty miles of sand and cactus. Besides, they'd leave tracks a blind man could follow. They obviously took the van someplace where they could take their time with the doors, and not risk scattering the cargo with an overcharge."

"Okay. I'll buy the reason for taking the whole van. That answers the why. What about the how?"

"Do you ever read Sherlock Holmes stories?" Fowler said.

"Nope, and I don't read Secret Agent X, or the Shadow, or any of those other super detectives. I see too many crooks every day on the job to want to entertain myself with them at home."

"I read Holmes. Sometimes I learn a thing or two about deduction. Sir Arthur Conan Doyle, Holmes' creator hit on a fundamental truth when he wrote: 'Once you eliminate the impossible, whatever remains, no matter how improbable, must be the truth.'"

"I'm an Ockham's Razor man myself," Cooper said around a mouthful of baked potato. "The simplest solution to a problem is most likely the correct one. You're still thinking it was a skyhook snatch, aren't you?"

"The Germans used zeppelins for aerial bombing in the War. And our side used them to airdrop artillery and vehicles into combat zones, at least on a limited scale. If an airship could pick up a tank, it could pick up an armored van with a sling, a loading fork or some other apparatus."

"But something as big as a blimp, wouldn't people see it?"

"In the middle of nowhere in the middle of the night, maybe not."

"Okay, I'll buy the possibility. Next question, what do we do about it?"

"We have to assume this van is gone and we're not going to find it any time soon, if ever. We can also assume that since they were successful, they'll do it again."

"That's a lot of assuming," Cooper said.

"At this stage, what else have we got? We could wait for them to strike again, or we could set a trap to catch them in the act."

"You got something in mind?"

Fowler nodded. "Yeah, as a matter of fact, I do."

Whitlock Transport's offices were located ten miles outside Denver in a desert compound that included three huge warehouses; a parking area with an assortment of tractor trailers, panel trucks and armored vans, an office building, and a service garage with doors tall enough to admit the biggest of the trucks, all enclosed in a ten-foot chain link fence topped with barbed wire. It was nine-thirty in the morning, and Fowler was surprised he couldn't see his breath in the air, it felt so cold. Cooper's boss, Assistant Director Paul Travers badged them past the guard at the gate house and was directed to the office building.

As they drove across the compound, Fowler took note of the fence and the night lighting. The lights, incandescent spots on twelve-foot poles, were more heavily concentrated in the area where the company vehicles were parked, leaving much of the fenced perimeter in shadow. Of course, the company didn't store money on site, and the most valuable thing it had to protect were its vans and trucks.

The offices were housed in a blunt cinder block building that was as artfully executed as a breadbox, obviously designed by the same architect who envisioned the warehouses and maintenance garage. They looked for all the world, as if they had been made intentionally ugly.

Inside, it looked like any office building with plastered walls and tiled floors that made the grit from outside grind under their feet. A receptionist's desk in the foyer offered a pleasant young woman with dark hair, who greeted the agents with a broad smile.

"Good morning, Miss," Travers said. "I am Deputy Director Travers of the FBI. We're here to see Mister Whitlock."

"Yes, sir; you're expected. Follow me, please."

They climbed the stairs to the second floor and were ushered past a secretary into an office with a desk in front of a window that offered a panoramic view of the truck lot. At the desk sat a bullet headed man in shirtsleeves with the knot of his tie pulled down and his collar open.

"Mister Whitlock, these are the gentlemen from the FBI."

Albert Whitlock, the owner and President of Whitlock Transport was red-faced to the crown of his bald head and gruff for the first thirty seconds of the meeting with the agents. "I want to know what the hell you people are doing about this robbery." His glare swept the three of them.

Travers said, "Mister Whitlock, we ..."

Fowler put up his hand and interrupted Cooper's boss. "Let's start off on the right foot, Whitlock," Fowler said. "The car's got only one steering wheel, and I'm the driver. You make no demands of us, we make them of you. I intend to solve this case, and it will happen on the Bureau's dime and on the Bureau's schedule. You are not in charge, you will not dictate to us or our personnel, and we, not you, will ask the questions. Understood?"

Whitlock glared and tried to stare Fowler down without success. He turned to Travers. "Are you going to let this underling speak to me like that?

Travers nodded his head. "Yes, I suppose I am."

"I asked you a question, Whitlock," Fowler snarled. "Do you understand the terms of this operation?"

"Yes," Whitlock hissed through his teeth.

"Yes, Agent Fowler."

Whitlock fumed but relented. "Yes, Agent Fowler."

"Much better. Now Agent Cooper will ask you some questions. When he's finished, I'll tell you how we're going to proceed. We all want the same thing: to solve this case. Keep that in mind. Agent Cooper?"

Cooper reached into his briefcase and pulled out a flip over steno book and a pencil. "So, Mister Whitlock, how many employees does your company have?"

"Forty-two, including office staff."

"And who decides what routes your deliveries from the Mint follow?"

"My logistics manager Roger Colley. Three routes are all carefully planned for any high risk shipments to minimize exposure and maximize efficiency. Then one hour before the shipment leaves the source, the choice is made which route the van will follow."

"And Roger Colley—how long has he worked for you?"

"Twelve years, eight in his current position."

"Okay. Colley decides on the route. Who else knows what it will be?"

"Ron Davis, my operations manager, and Mick Barber, my head of security."

"And you have no knowledge of the chosen route?"

"We run as many as twenty-five shipments a day, from small packages to trailer loads of goods. I'm not personally involved in every one of them. That's why I hire people."

"And how is this information conveyed to the drive team?"

"By a coded telephone call. Colley and Barber can explain it to you."

"Tell us about the driver and the guard."

"Charlie Foster, Lou Bingham and Bill Henner. They've all been with me for years. They have clean records. I couldn't imagine any of them going bad."

"There's always a first time. We'll check them out. And have you fired any employees recently, or had any disputes that would leave people wanting revenge?"

"No. My employees are all loyal. I'd no sooner suspect one of them than fly to the moon."

"We're the exact opposite," Fowler said. "We suspect everybody. You included. I expect full cooperation and full access to your operation for the duration of this investigation. Will I have it?"

Whitlock ground his teeth. "Yes."

"Good. Now, we need to speak to," he looked at Cooper's notes. "Colley, Davis and Barber. Set it up." Whitlock was speechless.

As they left Whitlock's office, Travers said, "Do you always lead with your blackjack, Fowler?"

"A guy like Whitlock would interpret diplomacy as a sign of weakness. If we let him, he'd be sending us out for coffee. You guys have to work around here after this is over; I don't. I figured I could yank his wattles, then go back to D.C. He can be pissed off at me forever and it won't matter."

Travers nodded slowly. "Thanks, I think."

Whitlock Transport's Security offices were also on the second floor. A secretary led them into a room with a conference table and chairs. A pair of Stromberg fat-boy telephones sat at one end. Maps of the five-state area lined the walls, routes marked with string and push pins.

Cooper pointed to the half-open window blinds. "If somebody stood outside in the right spot, he could see these maps."

"But the routes aren't identified by their codes." The agents turned to see a man in a suit whose bulk filled the doorway. "I'm Mick Barber, Security Chief." Another smaller man followed him into the room. He was in work greens with the company name and the name Davis stitched over the shirt pocket. "Colley will be here in a minute."

The men took chairs around the table, Barber sitting at the head of the table by the phones, establishing his authority. "What do you want to know?"

"A lot. I'm Deputy Director Travers from the Bureau's Denver office. These are agents Fowler and Cooper. We're investigating the disappearance of your vehicle."

"Yeah, the Boss told us." Barber said.

Cooper opened his notebook. "Let's start with your protocol for selecting routes."

Colley, a balding man with a pot belly that strained his white shirt came in and took a seat at the table.

For the next half hour, the three explained the procedure they followed to choose a delivery route from city to city, and how the choice was made known

"I'm Mick Barber, Chief of Security."

to the team.

"We confer and make the decision jointly," Barber said, "and call the regional depot to give them the choice. The routes are coded by pairs of letters AR, BF, and so on."

"Any possibility there could be a tap on the phone?"

"Even if there were, the information would be useless," Davis said. "We change the route codes weekly."

"And who all has the code info?" Cooper asked. "How many people?"

"Me, Colley," he nodded at Davis, "and Ron."

"Then how do the drivers know which is which?"

"The driver has three possibilities," Colley explained. "The final choice arrives a few minutes before departure time."

Barber shrugged, his shoulders straining his suit. "It's worked pretty well 'til yesterday."

Travers said, "We will need to review all of your personnel files."

"All of them?"

Travers nodded. "All the way up to Whitlock. That's enough for now, but we will be talking with you again as the investigation continues." He rose and the agents followed.

As they walked out the door, Barber said, "Hey Fowler." Dan turned. "You the same guy who broke up that counterfeiting ring in Virginia last year?"

"Yeah, that's me."

Barber nodded. "Thought so. I'm glad the Bureau is sending in the hotshots. I want this solved as much as you do. It could mean my job. I'll cooperate any way I can."

"Good. You can start right now," Fowler told him. "Give us permission to search this room."

On the ride back to Denver, the agents kicked around the info and what it might mean.

"Whitlock's route planning is a good example of Franklin's Rule," Fowler said.

"Franklin's Rule?"

"Benjamin Franklin in *Poor Richard's Almanac*: Three can keep a secret if two of them are dead."

"Choosing the route at the last minute makes it tough to plan an intercept," Cooper argued.

"But why the route codes?" Travers asked. "That seems like an extra layer of fat in the process."

"Seemed like a good idea when they started, and like Barber said, it's worked up to now."

Fowler broke in. "The whole procedure worked up to now. You can't isolate one gear in the works and give it credit or blame. Somehow, the info got into the crooks' hands. Find the leak, you'll find the crooks."

"Do you think it could be Barber, Colley, or Davis?" Travers said.

"First impression? No. But we need to take a closer look at them as we screen the other employees. It could be any of them or none of them."

"That conference room is anything but secure. Who knows who might be listening on the other side of the wall? I think they got complacent and let their guard down."

"What are you thinking, Dan?" Travers asked.

"I'm thinking we need to search the whole building."

"I'll have a warrant prepared."

Fowler nodded. "I'll keep it in my back pocket."

"What do you mean?"

"If we're dealing with an insider, and we walk in with a search team, he'll know immediately and shut down. We have to do this on the Q.T. Besides, I want to find out first-hand just how tight security is in that compound. Coop and I can sneak in at night and do a sweep, see what we find."

Travers was silent for a long time. Finally, he said, "The Director has every confidence in you, so I will too. I'll get the warrant. You two serve it however you see fit. I'm going to trust your judgment, Dan, and hope this doesn't blow up in our faces."

Back at the Bureau office, Travers made the call for the warrant. Cooper and Fowler went to lunch.

"I agree that the crooks had somebody on the inside, Dan, but if they did, they could have picked their target a little better. Who's going to waltz into a bank with a wheelbarrow full of shiny new halves? I mean, surely someone would notice. If it were me, I'd wait 'til they were shipping a load of paper money someplace and then make a move."

"That would make more sense. Maybe they plan on melting down the coins and selling the bulk silver."

"Another possibility. We're talking two and a half tons, give or take. By the time the silver is rendered, shipped and sold, the return wouldn't be nearly as great as the face value of the coins. They'd lose thirty percent or more. Maybe they didn't know it was all coin."

"That wouldn't make sense either," Fowler said. "If they had precise information about the route, they'd know that the shipment was coming from the mint, and it would have to be coin."

"Yeah, I see the point."

"So while your people do the legwork on Whitlock's employees, you and I have to pin down the leak in their security. So, tonight . . ."

For the next hour, Coop and Fowler fielded ideas and made plans for the evening's search of the Whitlock facility.

"I'll drop you at your hotel," Cooper offered.

"Yeah, I need to check in with the home office."

"I'll pick you up around midnight. Travers should have the warrant ready."

Ten minutes later, Cooper turned the corner at the Union Depot and pulled up in front of the Oxford Hotel, which billed itself as Denver's oldest. A liveried doorman held one of the double doors for Fowler as he stepped under the leaded glass fanlight from the bright afternoon sun into the cool shade of a lobby filled with leather chairs and sofas. He stepped to the desk for his key.

The clerk, a tall, rawboned character with a wing collar and a four-in-hand tie, handed him his room key and a folded piece of paper. "A message for you, Mister Fowler."

"Thanks." Fowler unfolded the paper as he headed for the elevator. It was from Sally Vane, his co-worker at the D.C. office and his "unofficial fiancée".

"Be careful, Dan. Call me. Sally."

Fowler smiled and slipped the note into his pocket. The bank of elevators stood to the left of the desk at the far end of the lobby. An operator in a brass buttoned uniform with epaulettes stood ready to take him upstairs. "Floor, sir?"

"Three please," he read the operator's brass name plate, "Eddie."

The little man grinned. "I appreciate that, sir. Most people look right through me. You're the first person this week to call me by my name."

Fowler returned the smile. "It costs nothing to be polite and respectful. My name's Dan."

The car stopped at Fowler's floor. "Nice to meet you, Dan. I'm on duty every day 'til midnight. If you need anything, ring for me."

"Thanks, I'll remember that."

Eddie slid the X cage closed. He pushed the button to clear his calls and turned the crank. The car disappeared down the shaft.

In his room, Fowler took off his hat and jacket and hung his shoulder rig on a chair beside the bed. The hotel operator answered in three rings and set about connecting him to a line to D.C. and the Bureau.

Fowler identified himself by badge number to the switchboard operator and asked to be connected to the Director. After a minute or so of clicks and hums, a familiar voice came on the line, Stone, the Director's personal assistant. "The Director's in a meeting, Fowler. He said you should make your report to me."

"All right, Stone, grab your pencil." For the next fifteen minutes, Fowler outlined the progress of the investigation. He left out the plan for the Midnight search of the Whitlock offices. "If there are questions or any directives for me, they can be forwarded to the Denver office."

The line went dead. That Stone; always the charmer. Fowler tapped the switch hook and the hotel operator answered. "This is Room 317. Would you connect me with the same number again, please?" This time, he asked for

Sally's extension.

Sally asked Fowler once why he never carried a photo of her in his wallet, and his reply was simple. "I don't need a picture. Your image is fixed in my mind for good." The real reason he didn't carry Sally's picture with him was that he didn't want her identity as an agent compromised, or for some crook to connect the two of them and use her to get to him.

Petite, blond, and athletic, Agent Vane was one of the first females to serve in the Bureau in that role, and her debutante image masked a thoroughly trained operative. More than one criminal had made the mistake of underestimating her skills in firearms and hand-to-hand combat.

Fowler kept their working relationship strictly business when they were on a case, but at other times, he saw Agent Vane as just Sally.

She answered on the second ring. "Agent Vane speaking."

"Agent Fowler here," Dan said with mock seriousness. They both laughed. "Busy day today, Sally?"

"Every day, Dan. You know that. How's Denver?"

"Hot in the day time and cold at night. They tell me it's the thin air."

"Is it harder to breathe?"

"I'm okay unless I sprint."

Sally laughed. "I know better than to tell you to take it easy."

They went on with some small talk, and finally, Sally said, "We'd better quit running up the Bureau's phone bill."

"You're right. I'll call tomorrow."

"You'd better. And Dan ..."

"Yeah. Sally?"

"Please be careful. You come home to me, you hear?"

"I hear and obey," Fowler said with a laugh. "And you be careful too. No jaywalking."

Fowler hung up smiling.

Cooper rang Fowler's room at twelve thirty. "Travers got us the warrant. Ready to roll?"

"Yeah. I'll go out the back of the hotel and walk around the block to the Union Depot. I'll wait inside the main entrance."

"I'll be in the same car I was in today. See you in a half hour."

Fowler hung up the phone and slipped into his shoulder rig. He dropped the clip from his .45 and checked the load, put it back in the pistol and racked a shell into the chamber. He slid the automatic into the holster, put on a waist length jacket, picked up a small leather satchel and headed for the door.

He took the fire stairs rather than be seen coming and going by the elevator operator. On the ground floor, he followed the corridor leading to the rear entrance of the hotel. The doors opened to an alley wide enough to accommodate the daily parade of delivery and garbage trucks. It was better lit than average, but Fowler saw no need to slink through the shadows.

He was dressed in dark chinos and a work shirt under a jacket zipped against the evening chill, a snap brim cap pulled down to his ears. His black brogans were steel capped under the leather. Fowler looked like any working stiff coming off a shift; the few people he passed didn't look twice.

At the Depot, he bought a newspaper and a pack of Lucky Strikes and settled down on one of the church-pew benches where he could see the street to wait for Cooper. The Senate rejected FDR's proposal to enlarge the Supreme Court, Amelia Earhart was still missing, and the Japanese, who attacked the Marco Polo Bridge, invading China a few days before, were pushing deeper. Halfway through the sports page, Cooper pulled up and Fowler left the paper and all the bad news on the bench.

Cooper was dressed in a black turtleneck sweater under a dark sport jacket.

Fowler snorted. "You look like a blond Robert Taylor."

"I'll take that as a compliment." He patted an envelope on the seat beside him. "There's the warrant. Travers is still edgy about this, you know."

"Tell him, '*Qui audet adpiscitur.*'"

"My Latin's rusty."

"'He who dares wins.'"

"Oh yeah? You tell him."

"If we get caught, we're still legal. We just knocked and nobody answered."

"Let's do our best to not get caught, how about it."

"No argument here."

"What's in the bag? Salami sandwiches?"

"Tools of the trade. You brought yours, didn't you?"

Cooper nodded. "Sure did. Wouldn't leave home without them."

Cooper switched off the crackling short wave and turned on the car radio, which crackled almost as much as it warmed up. Guy Lombardo's version of "September in the Rain" faded in, and the song made Fowler think of Sally, and the last time he'd taken her dancing.

He'd taken her to the Mayfair, "The Cafe of All Nations," at 13th and F Street, the club with the mural over the bar picturing men carrying the flags of a dozen countries. The Mayfair was a favorite of theirs because the food was good, the floor show was entertaining, and the place was big enough for anonymity, but small enough to be remembered by the *maître d'* and the wait staff, who on more than one occasion discreetly summoned Dan to the telephone for an urgent call from the Bureau.

Sally looked especially beautiful that evening, her hair swept back and held by a tortoise comb, her bare shoulders rising like soft dunes from her evening dress, glowing in the multicolored light. When Jack Campbell played the intro to "September in the Rain," Sally had grabbed Dan's hand and said, "I love this song. Dance with me."

They glided around the floor, and as the song was about to move to its final chorus, Dan caught the pianist's eye and made a rolling motion with his forefinger behind Sally's back. Campbell winked and extended the song, and the moment.

Sally said softly in his ear, "I wish it could always be like this, Dan. Nobody else in the world but you and me."

"Yeah, that would be great." They'd had the conversation many times before and it always ended the same way. They agreed that Sally had worked too hard and overcome too much opposition to become an agent, and while the Bureau might turn a blind eye to their relationship, it likely would not allow her to maintain her status if they ever married.

The song ended, and Dan stepped up to the dais to speak to Campbell. "Thanks, Jack." He slipped a five into the pianist's palm.

"Happy to oblige, Dan. I'm a big fan of romance."

He and Sally returned to their table, and Dan ordered another round of drinks. He'd nearly lost her more than once in the course of their cases together, and she him. They treasured these islands of peace in a sea of violence, and he wanted this one to last just a little longer. Sally folded his hand into hers, and her look told him everything he ever needed to know.

"Did you hear me?" Coop said. "Barber, Davis, and Colley all look clean so far. Nothing big on their records, a few cat and dog things, an assault charge against Barber, a D-and-D on Davis; all misdemeanors."

"How about the Boss, Whitlock?"

Not a blemish. Of course if he had, his company wouldn't be hauling for the Mint."

"Right. Time to look at the smaller fish."

Cooper pulled the Ford to the side of the road a half mile from the Whitlock compound, whose stark lights they could see in the distance. "We hoof it from here."

They knew from their review of security procedures earlier in the day that the compound had a two-man team who patrolled the fence line around its perimeter every two hours, night and day. "If we run into anybody, badges first."

"Unless they start shooting."

"Let's go," Cooper said.

The sand made for a tricky slog in the darkness. "I have to be careful where I put my feet," Fowler said quietly. "It's too easy to turn an ankle."

"You should have worn boots," Cooper said. "More ankle support and you can tuck your trouser cuffs into them to keep out critters."

"Critters?"

"Scorpions and spiders. Maybe tuck your trousers into your socks."

"Good idea."

What would have been a ten minute walk on pavement took the agents more than a half hour. As they neared the compound, they saw the guards on their round in tandem, one inside the fence and the other outside. Their flashlights bobbed around a corner of the fence and disappeared.

Fowler and Coop had to be more careful as they neared the perimeter. They chose the northwestern corner where the bank of warehouses blocked a wide area from view. They chose a section where they could straddle a pole, giving them more support than a swaying middle area. The climb was easy enough, and at the top, Cooper laid a hide spilt of tanned latigo over the barbed wire to allow him to roll over it and drop to the other side. Fowler followed, and they moved into the stark shadows cast by the lights. Fowler motioned to circle left around the nearest warehouse, and in a few moments they were at the rear entrance of the office building.

Fowler crouched at the door and picked the lock in less than a minute. They stepped inside and found the building dead quiet. Upstairs, they found the office doors locked. Cooper took Colley's office and Fowler took Barber's.

For a security chief, Barber seemed pretty lax. Neither his desk drawers nor his filing cabinet were locked. Rifling the files produced nothing but ordinary paperwork. The top left drawer of Barber's desk held the accessories of an earlier time in his career: two sets of brass knuckles, one plain and one with knobs, a spring black jack covered in braided leather, and a switchblade knife. The right hand drawer held a loaded .38 revolver and a box of shells.

Fowler picked up the telephone, a Stromberg-Carlson dial phone and turned it over, careful to keep the handset in the cradle to prevent the line opening in case the company had an operator on duty at night. A quick look told him there was nothing odd in the phone. He set it down and raised Barber's desk blotter. Nothing. Fowler carefully replaced the blotter and the phone and pushed the lock button on Barber's door set. As he was stepping into the hall, Cooper was closing the door to Colley's office.

Together, they went into the conference room, whose door was unlocked. "Great security," Cooper said. He tugged at the window blind cord and the slats closed, shutting out the compound lights.

"Anything in Colley's office?" he said quietly.

Cooper shook his head. "Nothing out of order that I could see."

"Same with Barber's office. Let's see what we find in here."

The conference room had two of the same type of telephone as Barber's office. Fowler examined each in its turn, unscrewing the mouthpiece and the earpiece in each handset, looking for hidden microphones or transmitters. Again, he was disappointed. They turned the hard oak chairs upside down and went so far as to move the table to one side while they rolled back the rug to examine the floor underneath. Again, nothing.

When they set the table back in place, being careful to put the legs in the dents in the rug, Fowler crawled under it to take a close look at the underside. He shined his flashlight under the table top. Three of the legs were glued in place. The fourth was held by a pair of shiny brass screws. "Coop," he whispered, "give me a screwdriver."

They tilted the table and put a chair under it to lift it clear of the rug. Fowler undid the long screws that held the top of the table leg in place. When the leg came away, Fowler saw wires leading into a hollowed out recess in the table top. He pulled gently and a black cylinder emerged attached to a battery and a microphone.

Cooper whistled softly.

Fowler put a finger to his lips and slid the apparatus back into the hole. He fitted the leg back in place and whispered, "Don't talk. Somebody may be listening." He quickly replaced the bug and screwed the table leg back in place. He motioned Cooper to follow him. In the hall, he said, "Okay, we know the how, not the who."

"And we're back to the start again. The room was open to anyone, so anyone could have put it there."

"But maybe we can use the crooks' ear to lay a snare."

"Now all we have to do is get out of here without getting caught." Cooper looked at his watch. "The guards will be passing our exit point in eighteen minutes. Do you feel lucky?"

Fowler shook his head. "I say we play it safe and wait 'til they're done with their round." He sat on the floor and leaned against the wall. "Have a seat."

"Poke me if I snore."

On the way back to Denver, Cooper said around his cigarette, "So who do we tell what?"

Fowler rubbed his chin. "That's a tough call. We can use the bug to lay a trap if we play it right, but we have to make a judgment call as to whom we can trust."

"Barber?"

"He's a candidate. But I want to wait until we brace Colley before we make that decision."

"Agreed. What about Davis?"

"It'll be hard to lay a trap without him knowing. We'd need his help and his silence."

"I still think your plan is a big risk all around."

"Got any better ideas?"

"Let me sleep on it."

A little before sunrise, Bill Perkins and Milo Swift put their rowboat into the water. Banger's Lake had a formal name on the maps, but none of the locals ever used it. The moniker came from its popularity as a trysting spot for the area's teens. It also was one of the best spots in the county to fish for rainbow trout and largemouth bass.

"Oughta be a good day to fish," Milo said, loading his gear into the back of the boat.

"Don't say that. You'll jinx us for sure."

"Hey, look." Milo pointed to a bass floating on its side nearby. He waded into the lake with a net and scooped it out of the water. "Damn," he said. "Not quite trophy size." He hefted it in the net. "I'd say six, maybe seven pounds."

"Throw him back," Bill said. "Maybe he'll be big enough next season."

"There's another one."

"See any more?"

Milo scanned the surface of the lake. "Nope."

"Then let's get out there while there's still a few live ones."

Fifty feet from shore, Milo threw out the anchor and the pair hunkered down for some serious fishing.

The morning turned out to be a disappointment. Milo caught three bass, none over five pounds, and Bill caught one. "Told you you'd jinx us," Bill grumbled. He pulled at the anchor rope, and it wouldn't budge. "And now the anchor's caught, too. Gimme the 'see bucket.'"

Milo handed Bill the glass-bottomed bucket for underwater viewing. Bill put it in the water and peered through the bottom. "Holy Moses, Milo, look at this." In the dim light of the lake bottom, Milo made out the pumpernickel shape of an armored van.

Two hours later, Fowler, Cooper, and Barber stood on the shore of Banger's Lake as a pair of tow trucks dragged the armored car out the water.

"I'd complain about the Sheriff's men mucking up the crime scene," Cooper said, "but according to him, except for the tire tracks of the fishermen's car there wasn't a mark on the shore."

"So they didn't drive it or tow it here." Fowler shaded his eyes and looked across the lake. "How deep is it?"

"Chest height to about thirty feet out, then the bottom slopes to about fifteen feet, maybe a little deeper in the middle."

"So they couldn't drive it fifty feet into the lake, either." Fowler looked to the sky. "However improbable . . ."

The tow trucks started their winches. The cables went as tight as a guitar string, and the motors strained as the sucking mud refused to let the truck

"Oughta be a good day to fish,"

go without a fight. Then, as if it changed its mind, it suddenly let go, and the cables started winding on the drums.

In a moment, the armored car heaved out of the water, leaving deep ruts in the shoreline mud.

"They left it in gear," Fowler said.

Cooper snorted. "Or left the parking brake on."

Fowler peered through the driver's window and saw the cab was half filled with water. He tried the door handle and found it locked. "Barber, the keys."

The security chief unlocked the door and pulled it open. Water gushed out, and a uniformed body tumbled to the ground. Barber rolled it over. "It's Charlie Foster." Inside the cab, Lou Bingham's body lay half under the dashboard.

The rear doors were twisted, likely blown open with nitro. Inside, Fowler and Cooper found Bill Henner's body on the floor of the cargo hold. His mouth was contorted in a rictus of agony.

"Do you see any bullet holes?" Cooper said.

"None in any of them. I see only one." Fowler's eyes drifted to the ceiling. He turned to the Sheriff. "We'll need to have these bodies autopsied immediately. Our people will take them."

"Welcome to 'em," the Sheriff said. "Damnedest thing I ever saw."

"And Sheriff, tell those men," Fowler nodded at Perkins and Swift, "they'd better not eat those fish they caught til we've checked out the dead ones."

"This is crazy," Barber said. "How could the truck end up in the bottom of a lake fifty feet from shore? Okay, I can see Bill killed when they blew the doors open, but his revolver was still in the holster. What about Charlie and Lou? Did they drown? What do you guys think?"

"We don't think anything til we have something to think about," Fowler said. "We'll know more after the autopsies. Word will get around fast that we found the truck. That's bad enough. Don't make it worse by running your mouth about it. Don't discuss any details with anyone."

Barber looked stung, but agreed. They left him staring into the cargo hold and headed back to the office.

Cooper stopped at a gas station to fill the car, and Fowler bought a newspaper. The headline read: ARMORED CAR DISAPPEARS. He read the story out loud as they drove. The article was correct, as far as the reporter knew the few facts available, but it quickly turned into a thinly veiled editorial about the need for law and order and the perils of returning to the days of Al Capone and John Dillinger.

"If they only knew," Cooper said, "Those days aren't returning. They never really went away."

"Pretty much what we expected. This changes things. We can't do a fake transport run if it'll put the crew at risk."

"We could do a fake run with our people in the truck."

"I'd be willing to drive," Fowler said, "but remembering what happened to the escort cars, I'd hate to put agents in them."

"Whitlock hauls for a lot of people. Maybe the trucks deadhead without backup when they're going to pick up a cargo."

"I get you, Coop. We follow the protocol for an empty run, no escort, but we talk it up in the room with the bug as if the truck has a payroll or something else high value. We pass it off as a good target, and the crooks go after it. This operation must have cost somebody a bundle. They'll do it again."

"They won't blow up the truck and risk destroying the cargo," Cooper said. "If we ask them real nice, the Army Air Corps could have a few dogfighters in the air far enough away to be out of sight but still in radio contact."

"And if we limit the people at Whitlock Transport who are in on the dodge, we'll narrow the field for who may be feeding the crooks info."

"And if the crooks don't take the bait?"

"Then we have to find the airship. It's the only way they could have pulled off the robbery."

"We've done aerial surveillance over a twenty-five hundred square mile area of nothing surrounding the crime scene. Surely we would have seen a blimp."

"That covers a fifty by fifty mile area. Most airships can travel two hundred miles a day. Maybe the search didn't range far enough. Were they looking in the air or on the ground?"

"Both. They were looking primarily for any sign of the armored van."

"We'll have to throw out the net, check for any reports of an airship in a hundred mile radius. If it flew during daylight, surely someone would have seen it. If not, then it went to ground before dawn. But again, someone should have seen it parked. How do you hide a dirigible?

"I think we can rule out the Grand Canyon. Maybe we didn't look far enough. Or close enough. Does the office have topographic maps of the area?"

An hour later, Fowler and Cooper had covered a conference table with overlapping U.S. Geological Survey maps for a forty thousand square mile area. "We're looking for any geological features that are big enough to hide an airship," Cooper told the agents who came in to help them. "Canyons, ravines, valleys between mountains, anything where an airship could hide."

An afternoon's search yielded six possibilities. Two canyons were not only wide enough but deep enough to swallow a full-sized airship. Four valleys between mountain ridges were also possibilities. "We still have three hours of daylight," Cooper told one of the agents. "Call the airfield."

An hour later, Fowler and Cooper were flying over the desert in a Piper J-2. Cooper manned the yoke while Fowler scanned the area below with binoculars and at each of the sites on the map saw plenty of nothing but sand and cacti.

"It looks as if we're coming up empty," Fowler said over the drone of the engine. "I guess we have to try another angle. Unless you have a better idea. We'll have to go for the fake delivery."

An hour later, Cooper had Colley in one interrogation room and Fowler was in another briefing Barber. "So, that's how the route information was stolen. Do you have any idea who might have planted the bug?"

Barber shook his head. "None. I'm mortified. I might as well turn in my resignation to Whitlock tomorrow, 'cause he'll ask for it as soon as he hears about this."

"Not so fast," Fowler said. "There's a way we might use this to catch the bastards, and you'll come out of this looking good."

"How?"

"By sending an empty truck as bait, but we'll be at the wheel, and when they strike, so will we."

"'When' they strike? You mean 'if', don't you?"

"This one will be too good to pass up."

The plan was tricky, but Fowler was hopeful. Colley, Barber, and Davis sat in the conference room and read from a prepared script.

"Can't we just hold onto the money and wait til this robbery is solved?" Davis said.

"No can do," Barber replied. "It has to be delivered to the bank by eight tomorrow. Our best bet is to treat it as a deadhead pickup run to fool the robbers; no escort cars, just like we would hauling empty."

"I don't like it," Colley said. "It puts our people at too much risk."

"You want to argue the point with the boss? He says do it. Besides, it's three people involved, not nine."

"It's over a hundred grand. Can we afford to take that chance?" Colley said.

"It's not our decision. The run'll start at eleven tonight, so we'll meet here at ten-thirty to set the route. And I'll be driving the van."

"You?" Colley said. "More power to you. I'm glad it's not me."

They stepped into the hallway where Fowler and Cooper were waiting.

"Good work," Cooper said. "I hope they were listening."

Fowler added, "And they tune in tonight."

When they returned to the office, the autopsy report on Charlie Foster was sitting on Cooper's desk. Coop opened the folder and began scanning the first page. "Holy Moses!"

"What is it?"

"Foster, the van driver died of poisoning. Cyanide."

"Somebody slipped poison in his coffee?"

"It wasn't in his stomach, it was in his lungs. They gassed him."

"I'm guessing that happened after they got the van stopped. That's probably how the other two with him died."

"We'll know for sure tomorrow when the other reports come in," said Cooper. "Makes sense. They can't shoot into the truck without opening it up, and then if they did, Whitlock's men would start shooting back."

"Just drill a hole in the truck, pump the gas in with a hose, and wait," Fowler said, recalling the hole in the truck's roof.

"If they were using gas, they could have just knocked them out." Cooper picked up the phone.

"These boys play for keeps. Who are you calling?"

"The National Guard Armory to see whether they can spare a couple of gas masks. We might need them tonight."

Fowler's shoulders were too broad for the first Whitlock uniform shirt he tried on, so he went for the next size. The starched white shirts were tricked out with epaulets and creases stitched into the fabric. Navy blue trousers, a peaked hat with a patent leather visor and a badge with the words "Whitlock Transport" completed the uniform. Fowler substituted his automatic for the Colt revolver in the Sam Browne belt.

"We look official," Cooper said.

Just then Barber came in wearing the same uniform.

"What's this?" Fowler said.

"I'm riding with you."

Cooper and Fowler exchanged a look.

"Says who?"

"These aren't nickel and dime robbers we're dealing with. If there's trouble, you'll need an extra gun. Besides, you've never driven one of our trucks, I have. Most of all, some of the men those rats killed were friends of mine. I want to help take them down."

Fowler nodded. "Okay, Barber, you're in."

Cooper opened his mouth to protest, but a look from Fowler cut him off. Then to Barber, "Go set the route with Colley and Davis. Coop and I will be out in a minute."

As soon as Barber was out of earshot, Cooper said, "What are you thinking? He's a suspect. He could shoot us both when things go down."

"Not if he's in the lockup, he can't. I have a little surprise for Barber. I'm driving, not him. If he's in the cargo hold, he can't get a signal out with a radio, thick as the steel plate is."

"I guess you're right," Cooper said. "If he is in on it, it's better to have him shut in the box."

"My thinking exactly."

The transport truck was waiting in the service bay along with Barber, Colley, and Davis.

Fowler set down a canvas knapsack. "What are you carrying?" he asked Barber.

"My service revolver and that riot gun," he said, pointing to the .12 gauge leaning against the side of the truck.

"That's good. You'll need it if they break into the cargo hold. That's where you'll be riding."

"What?" Barber started shaking his head. "No, no. No way. You can't drive this heap."

"Believe it or not, I can. I've driven them before, and just about everything else with wheels. This is our show, Barber, not yours. We make the decisions, we give the orders. Cooperate, or you'll spend the whole time we're gone hand-cuffed to that railing over there."

Barber tried staring Fowler down, and found it didn't work. He thought things over for a few seconds, grabbed the shotgun by the slider and climbed into the truck.

Fowler reached into the knapsack and pulled out a gas mask. "Catch." He tossed it into the cargo hold to Barber. "You might need this, push come to shove. Turns out your men in the truck were killed with poison gas."

"Poison gas? Wait! Wait!"

Fowler slammed the door. It had a dual security system, a lock on the out-side, and one on the inside. As he turned the key in the outer lock, he saw Barber staring through the plate of bulletproof glass, a look of fear in his eyes. He could set the inside lock, or not. Fowler didn't care.

He stepped on the starter, and the van's engine rumbled into life. "Ready, Coop?"

"Let the good times roll."

Colley came to the passenger window with a shopping bag.

"What's this?" Cooper said.

"Sandwiches and coffee. You said to make this look like any regular run in case somebody was watching."

"Thanks. It's all in the details."

Colley stepped back, and with a grinding of gears, the armored van rolled forward.

"I thought you said you drove these before."

"Once a couple of years ago. I never said I drove it well."

"Time to check on our backup." Cooper switched on a portable short wave radio. The frequency was open to a carload of agents who would follow the van at a discreet distance and to a pair of Air Corps pilots in Curtis Shrikes who would fly a parallel course, ready to swoop in at the first sign of trouble. Their Browning machine guns would make the fight a tad more even. In a moment, connections were confirmed, and all went to radio silence.

The radio operator at Whitlock's base said someone jammed the radio signal the night the truck was robbed. If that happened again, Fowler was ready to fire flares that would be seen by the pilots and the backup car. Help would arrive quickly.

Cooper looked through the glass into the cargo hold. Barber was sitting on a fold down jump seat staring at the gas mask in his lap.

"Can he hear us?" Fowler said.

"Between the engine noise and thick glass, I'd say no."

"For what it's worth, Coop, I don't think Barber's the insider."

"Why's that?"

"When he insisted on driving, I had my suspicions, but then I mentioned the poison gas. It took him by surprise. He's genuinely scared."

"So that leaves Davis and Colley."

"And everyone else on Whitlock's payroll, unfortunately. Pour me a cup of coffee, will you. It's going to be a long ride."

The armored car rolled through the night at a steady forty-five miles an hour without interruption. By the end of three hours, their nerves were frayed by the constant on-edge anticipation. On one hand, they wanted the robbers to make a move, and on the other, they were relieved that they'd live to see the sun come up.

"I'm okay in an airplane," Cooper said, "but I wouldn't feel comfortable cruising in a flying gas bomb. I keep thinking about the Hindenburg going down in flames.

"If it is a zeppelin, it's probably filled with helium."

"It works the same?"

"Almost as well. You lose a little lift, but it's a fair trade. Helium is an inert gas. It won't burn or mix with other elements. It is relatively expensive, though, much rarer than hydrogen. Any kid can separate hydrogen from oxygen."

"Yeah, I remember that from chemistry class in high school, trapping them in separate bottles. You hold a match to the hydrogen bottle and it pops like a little explosion."

Fowler nodded. "We don't sell helium to Germany any more, thanks to Harold Ickes. After the Krauts annexed Austria, he pushed for a ban on helium sales. The other cabinet members disagreed, but he was such a hard ass about it that FDR let him have his way. It sent a message. Of course, where there's a need, money always finds a way to fill it."

"The cost of this operation doesn't seem to outweigh the rewards," Cooper said. "Unless they plan to do it again and again."

Like tonight."

Fowler nodded. "Like tonight."

The ride out was uneventful. They waited a half hour at the turnaround as if they were unloading, and started the three hour drive back.

"Looks like this is a bust," Cooper said, disgusted. "Nobody took the bait, and a hundred Gs is a big incentive."

"It suggests a few possibilities. Maybe we missed a leak somewhere. Or maybe the bad guys folded up and went home."

"Maybe they were afraid to hit the same line twice in a week."

"Or, crazy as it sounds, they didn't want bills. Maybe they just wanted the coins."

"Why in the world would somebody want a ton of half dollars?"

"Two thousand five hundred sixty-two point five pounds to be exact. Solve that one, Sherlock, and you'll be Director in no time."

"Should we call off the air support?"

"I suppose so. If the crooks knew this was a dummy run, they had no reason to snatch us. They already had one empty truck and dropped it in the lake. I don't imagine they want another one."

Cooper looked into the cargo hold again. Barber hadn't moved. "Do you think Barber's learned his lesson?"

"I'd say so. At the turnaround, he was so scared, I was afraid he might run away instead of getting back in the truck and we'd have to catch him and cuff him. He'll know next time to let the adults do their job. He won't interfere again."

"I'll be glad to get out of this uniform," Cooper said, scratching his armpit. "It's like wearing a cardboard box."

Fowler waited until seven to call Sally, figuring she'd be awake by then. She answered on the second ring. "It's about time you called, Dan. I hardly slept last night."

"Sorry, Sally. No phones in an armored car."

She understood that Fowler couldn't give her details over the telephone, so Sally didn't press for an explanation. "Since you're walking and talking, you must be okay."

"So far. How are things at the office?"

"Tedious. Just run of the mill stuff; kidnapping, murder, hijacking. Nothing interesting."

Fowler laughed. "Yes, yes," he drawled in his best W. C. Fields imitation. "The highways are fraught with marauders."

"All you need is a straw boater and a big red nose." Her voice turned serious. "Be careful, Dan. I want you to come back in an airplane, not in a hearse."

"I'd tell you not to worry, but I know better. In a few days this'll all be over and I'll take you to the Blue Flame for a steak. You can wear that red dress I like so much."

"Lady in red, huh?" The playfulness returned to her voice. "You saw how that turned out for Dillinger."

"Yeah, but we aren't going to the movies."

"No, the one we're in is bad enough. Gotta go, Dan. No tolerance for tardiness."

"Okay, Sally. I'll call tonight."

"Do that. I'll be staring at the phone."

He hung up, and stretched out on the bed. Sally's face was the last thing in his mind as he drifted off to sleep.

Albert Pender paced the floor of his apartment. The call had come an hour ago. Finally the man he knew only as Benz was going to deliver his money. Gambling was a slippery slope. Pender was way ahead, working his system then his luck turned, and suddenly he owed big money to some very unforgiving people. It was tricky to embezzle five thousand dollars from Whitlock, and it would be even trickier to put it back without getting caught, but he could make it work.

No more horses, he thought. I've learned my lesson.

When the knock came he still started, even though he expected it.

Pender opened the door to find Benz standing in the dark hallway holding a package the size of a brick wrapped in butcher paper and tied with twine. Benz stepped inside, and before Pender could close the door, a massive shape filled the doorway, a man whose face was a crazy canvas of livid scars. Pender tried to cry out, but Metz's huge hand clamped over his face and drove him across the room to pin him against the wall.

Benz closed the door.

The next morning passed with little movement on the case. At Travers' insistence, agents in pairs from Cooper's office questioned Whitlock's employees and found, to no one's surprise, that almost all had legitimate alibis for the night of the robbery. One pair, a driver and a secretary, when pressed, finally admitted that each was the alibi for the other, and, "please don't tell my spouse."

"Half down and half to go," Fowler said. "I really don't think questioning Whitlock's people will get us very far, Coop. I don't imagine any of them knocked over the van."

"You're probably right, but somebody planted the bug, and that required access to the building when no one was around. Besides, Travers insists we follow investigative protocol. Who knows? We might get lucky."

"Once we finish the initial interviews, we can get a polygraph operator in here to screen the most likely candidates."

"I don't like using a lie detector," Cooper said, "but sometimes the intimidation factor scares people into giving themselves away. Less work than beating it out of them."

"I suppose it's better than sitting around. It's Newton's First Law of Motion. Familiar with it?"

"Physics one-o-one: A body at rest remains at rest unless acted on by an outside force."

"And the corollary: a body in motion will remain in motion in a straight line unless acted upon by an outside force. That's a simplified version, but it shows the principle. We're dealing with inertia."

"Inertia?"

"Ever push a stalled car?"

Cooper chuckled. "Are you kidding? More times than I can remember."

"You grunt and strain and slowly, the wheels start to turn, and it picks up a little speed, and finally, inertia kicks in. You can just stroll behind the car with one hand on the boot, and it'll keep rolling as long as you keep applying force. Inertia keeps it rolling. If you stop feeding energy, the car stops, and you have to grunt and strain all over again to get it moving."

"So, you're saying as long as we keep active on the case, it keeps moving forward."

"More or less."

"Then I guess we just keep on pushing."

Fowler and Cooper interviewed the company's upper management while the other agents questioned the drivers and other staff. After lunch, they were scheduled to interview Albert Pender, Chief Accountant. Cooper eyed the photo in Pender's personnel file; dark hair parted in the middle, glasses with heavy black frames, and a sour look on his face.

"Looks like Harold Lloyd," Cooper said.

"Yeah, he does. He's ten minutes late already. I'll call downstairs and get him up here." Fowler went through the switchboard and got Pender's secretary on the phone. "This is Agent Fowler. Mister Pender was scheduled to meet with us. Please send him up."

Cooper heard the secretary's voice buzz in the earpiece. Fowler frowned. "I see. Just a moment." He put his hand over the mouthpiece. "Pender's secretary says he hasn't been in the office all day."

"Get his address from the secretary," Cooper said. "I'll bring the car around."

Pender lived alone in a walk up in a middle class suburb of Denver. The building was nestled between a grocer and a pharmacy on a fairly busy street.

Cooper looked up from the sidewalk and saw that one of Pender's windows was open. "What do you think, Dan?"

"Let's take a look around the block. I don't want him ducking out the back door while we're coming in the front."

A narrow brick alley, open at both ends ran parallel to the street. Pender's building had a street level exit door that opened onto a stairway.

"Hinges on the outside. The door swings into the alley. Bring the car around."

Cooper parked the sedan close enough to the building so that the exit door could swing only two or three inches.

"Hey! You can't park there. You're blocking the alley." The grocer, wearing a blood-stained butcher's apron, had stepped out for a smoke. He held his matches in one hand, and a cigarette in the other.

Cooper flashed his badge and put a hand on his hip, pushing back his coat and letting the storekeeper see his holstered automatic. "FBI," he snarled. "Get back inside and keep your mouth shut."

The grocer scurried back into the store.

"Now," Cooper said, "let's see if Pender's at home."

A light bulb at the top of the stairs was burnt out, and the narrow stairwell was dark once the street door was closed. The agents drew their weapons and climbed the stairs. Cooper took the lead, and at the landing, stood away from the door and knocked. "FBI, Mister Pender. Open the door."

He knocked again. No response. Cooper took off his hat and put his ear to the keyhole. "Sounds as if nobody's home but the flies."

"Flies?" Fowler kicked the door and splintered the frame. The door swung inward. Half the room was pristine and neat. The other was ghastly. Pender lay on the carpet, a shiny pistol in his hand. The back of his head was missing. The wall behind him looked as if someone threw a can of red paint at it. The blood had dribbled and dried on the *fleur de lis* wallpaper and the carpet where Pender's body lay. Dozens of flies buzzed around the corpse. A piece of his shattered dental plate lay beside him.

A slip of paper was thumb tacked to the wall. Written on it in a neat hand were the words, "I've embezzled money from the company. They'll catch me. I can't go to prison."

"So who do we call first?" Fowler said. "You have to work here after I'm gone. You know the local politics, I don't."

"I don't want to ruffle any official feathers. I'll call the local P.D. once my forensic team's on the way. The locals bitch about us 'interfering' and 'pulling rank,' but they never complain about the benefits."

"What do you think? Half an hour?"

"That should be enough time for a quick look. Any longer and the flies'll eat all the evidence."

They soon found Pender's motive for his part in the plot. A pile of racing forms and a ledger in his dresser drawer told the sad tale of a gambler with a "sure thing" system.

"Look at this," Cooper said. "Must be twenty pages of calculations in here.

"Hinges on the outside. The door swings into the alley."

It's all predictions and results. No money. He turned a few pages. "Here we go. He started playing the ponies last February." Cooper turned a few pages and whistled. "He was up twelve grand six months ago."

"Let me guess," Fowler said. "His luck jumped off the train."

"You got it. According to the last entry, he's down six Gs."

"That jibes with these." Fowler held out a wad of pawn tickets in a rubber band. "Looks as if he hocked everything loose the last few months."

Back in the living room, Fowler crouched to look at the chrome plated revolver in Pender's hand. "I don't like this, Coop, him holding the gun."

"You know the stats. Three quarters of gunshot suicides drop the piece. One quarter doesn't."

Fowler held Pender's sleeve between his thumb and forefinger. He lifted the arm carefully, studying the pistol at close range. "Immaculate."

"Huh?"

"Not a print or a smudge on the revolver." He put his handkerchief over his hand and pulled the ejector rod. The cylinder swung out. One spent cartridge; the rest were unfired. Fowler carefully drew out one of the unfired bullets. "The shells are clean. Why take the trouble to wipe down the gun and the shells if you're about to kill yourself? I'd bet a month's pay Pender didn't pull the trigger."

"I'd bet two month's pay you're right. I'll make the calls."

Later that afternoon an agent named Hutchinson tapped on the doorframe of Cooper's office. He was carrying one of the topo maps under his arm.

"Coop," Hutchinson said. "I was looking at the maps again, and I did find something that might hide a dirigible, but it's not just a hole in the ground." He tapped a spot on the map in front of him. "Castle Mesa. It may sound crazy, but this mesa might be able to hide a full sized airship. And it's only fifty miles from the hijacking scene."

"It doesn't sound any crazier than the thought of a dirigible snatching an armored car full of half dollars like a hawk grabbing a rabbit," Fowler said. "Show us."

Hutchinson pointed to a group of irregular concentric ovals that indicated a sharp rise in elevation, to approximately a hundred fifty feet from the desert floor on the Arizona side of the border, a mesa. In its center, the ovals reversed, indicating a crater.

Cooper held a magnifying glass over the map. "The contour lines don't look to go deep enough."

"Maybe it's been excavated," Hutchinson said. "Out there, who'd notice?"

"Good thinking, Hutch."

"Crazy as it seems," Fowler said, "however improbable . . ."

"What?"

"Our mistake has been thinking dirigible, with a rigid frame. We should have been thinking blimp."

"I get it," Cooper said. "If it's deflated enough, it could be hidden in a shallower space." He looked at his watch. "We've got hours of daylight left. Let's do a flyover."

Cooper flew the Piper in a wide arc around the mesa to avoid attracting undue attention from the ground.

"I love flying these babies. Sometimes I think the only reason the Agency hired me is my air training."

"I'm sure it comes in handy."

"Yeah," Cooper snorted, "every time some bigwig needs to get someplace in a hurry. I feel like the Army wasted its money training me for air combat. Got your belt buckled?"

Cooper twitched the stick, and the Piper went into a steep dive. He yanked back on the stick and the plane angled sharply upward. The Piper leveled off, and Cooper sent it into a barrel roll. He finished his performance with a three-sixty loop.

"Can I breathe now?" Fowler said.

Cooper laughed. "Gotta stay in practice, Dan."

"Did you say the Air Corps trained you, or some flying circus?"

"Get ready. The mesa's coming up on the left."

Castle Mesa was an imposing mound of rock, rising almost straight up from the desert like a giant fist. "I'll make one pass and circle back for a second, try to make it look casual. I don't want to chance three in case there is something there. Don't want to tip anybody off."

"Right." Fowler raised his binoculars.

Cooper made his first pass and was looping around for the second when Fowler said, "I think Hutch is in line for a commendation. The maps show a thirty foot crater in the mesa. There is no crater."

Coop peered through the windscreen. "You're right. The top's almost level."

"Don't make another pass. We've seen enough to justify a closer look. You're good with an airplane. How are you with a parachute?"

Parachuting at night was bad enough, but jumping in the blackness before moonrise seemed almost suicidal, so they opted to wait for moonrise. Fowler and Cooper sat harnessed and ready in the back of a military cargo plane as it flew over the desert. Cooper leaned back in his jumpsuit, eyes closed, a cigarette at the corner of his mouth. Fowler was nervous about jumping and busied his mind with the case.

He had been right. According to the fingerprint man, the only prints on

Pender's pistol were his own. The thumbtack that held the suicide note, however, had a partial print that didn't match. Definitely not suicide. Pender was killed to shut his mouth. They had a Who and a How. What they needed now was a Why.

Coop nudged him. "How many times have you jumped, Dan?"

"Twice in training. I hoped I'd never have to do it again."

"Two minutes to target, gentlemen." An Army Air Corps Sergeant stood beside the sliding door to the right of the fuselage. Fowler adjusted his goggles. "See you on the ground, Coop." The sergeant opened the door and they could hear the rush of air over the drone of the Douglas's engines.

"Don't land in a cactus patch," Cooper said. He jumped first and Fowler followed him. His chute popped open and as the sound of the plane faded, Dan found himself suddenly wrapped in quiet. The edge of the moon appeared to his left, and in its weak light, he saw the mesa below him. Right on target. He couldn't see Cooper but he was sure that he was close.

Fowler braced himself for the tuck and roll when he hit the ground, but instead of a hard landing, he felt the surface give and he bounced like he might on a trampoline. He felt Cooper land the way a spider feels a fly in its web. Fowler hurried out of his harness and dragged the chute with him across the heavy canvas until he felt solid ground under him.

"Coop," he hissed.

"Yeah," came a stage whispered reply.

In a moment the agents were hiding their chutes under a ledge of rock. They were nearly finished when they heard voices. In a moment, flashlights were crisscrossing the top of the mesa. Two men.

The agents crouched behind an outcropping as the lights circled the rim of the tarp. In a moment, they'd be spotted. Fowler drew his automatic and cocked the hammer. A dark shape darted from behind a boulder and ran for the lip of the mesa. There was a rattle of machine gun fire and the shape fell. The lights closed on it and Fowler saw that it was an antelope.

"Why'd you shoot it?" one of the men said. "It was running for the edge."

"And it would've come back later and we'd be out here again."

The voices retreated and Fowler saw a rectangle of light appear across the tarp. The men disappeared into it, and the light with them. Fowler carefully stepped to the edge of the tarp and lay on it, his lower body on the ground. He opened his clasp knife and gently pushed its tip through the painted canvas. He sawed back and forth, making a three inch cut and put his eye to the opening.

Harsh light shone from below. In it, he saw an airship moored inside a huge pit, like a cavity in a molar. He was right; the gas bag was two-thirds deflated, and sagging with rumples and folds. A crew of men were painting something on its side while others were busy loading crates into the gondola. Near the airship's tail, he saw a tall grey haired man giving orders. Beside him was a short, compact man with a bald head dressed in a black suit.

"This case gets stranger by the minute," Coop whispered.

"The answers are all below, and we won't find them sitting here."

They circled the tarp area and found the door in the rock. It was locked. Fowler worked the lock with a set of burglar's picks. It had taken the guards a good two minutes to respond when the agents had bounced on the canvas, so they were likely not waiting inside the door with guns drawn.

Cooper put his ear to it. After listening for a few seconds, he nodded and opened it a crack. Inside they found a tunnel-like set of steps cut into the rock leading downward into the crater. From below came the steady throb of machinery and the smell of diesel fuel and machine oil.

The agents picked their way carefully down the stairs until they reached a switchback. From the platform they saw the open cavern excavated in the red rock and the airship that filled most of the cavity. The angle of the klieg lights kept them unseen by the men working below.

Coop nudged Fowler. "Okay, we've got 'em cold. Do you want to yell 'You're under arrest', or shall I?"

A catwalk branched out from the landing and stretched the length of the hollow. "You get out of here and go for the cavalry. I'm going to stay and try to find out what's really going on. This is no simple heist."

"Okay, partner. It's a long walk to the rendezvous. I'd better get started." Cooper climbed the steps, and Fowler slipped onto the catwalk.

On the top of the mesa, Coop circled the rim to the eastern face, the relatively shallower grade as shown on the map. He started down the slope and found it was not only steep, but strewn with rocks from the size of a softball to the size of a pea. The descent was treacherous, and about a third of the way to the bottom, he lost his footing and started a rolling slide down the stony face. He came to rest at the foot of the mesa against the trunk of a Joshua tree.

Cooper's left ankle was badly sprained, but he considered himself lucky; neither of his arms or legs was broken. He took his bearings by the stars and limped around the east side of the mesa. A pale line of light showed around a canvas flap that covered a tunnel dug into the mesa's base. He pulled it aside and found cars and trucks.

Coop crept inside and saw a lone guard leaning on the fender of a stake side truck. The agent slipped up behind him and slugged him behind the ear with his pistol. The guard sagged to his knees and for safety's sake, Cooper slugged him again.

A quick inventory showed him two trucks with tires that would grace a farm tractor, two sedans, and a pair of Indian motorcycles with balloon tires for riding on the desert. Cooper crawled under engines and reached under hoods to slash fuel lines and plug wires. He chose one Indian with a sidecar to take some of the strain off his injured ankle and cut the tires of the other. Then, though the pain was severe, he grabbed the handlebars of the motorcycle like a cowboy bulldogging a steer and pushed it across the sand into the darkness.

A quarter mile from the mesa, Cooper jumped the kick starter with his good foot, and on the third try the engine roared into life. He climbed on, shifted into first gear, and took off slewing side to side, throwing a rooster tail of sand behind him.

Inside the mesa, Dan Fowler crept along the catwalk for a better view of what the men were painting on the side of the envelope. In three foot letters: Castle News Parade. They were going to pass the airship off as a newsreel camera blimp. He searched his mind for what he'd read in the papers that week. Where was there going to be news? Suddenly the pieces fell into place and his blood ran cold.

The President was going to appear in a motorcade in Topeka the next day, part of his "confidence tour," designed to assure Americans that the Depression was done and prosperity was returning. The trip was a thin excuse for FDR to campaign for a pair of incumbent politicians, one a Congressman and one a Senator to maintain Democratic control of both houses and grease the wheels for his agenda. Fowler had been part of a security detail for a similar event in D.C, the year before and recalled the enormous Presidential limousine, a stately Packard touring car with Secret Service agents standing on the running boards and a cluster of motorcycle cops around it.

He remembered, too, the throngs of cheering people who lined the sidewalks four and five deep, craning their necks for a look at their savior from poverty and despair. Any one of them might have charged the limousine with a gun or a knife and been shot dead by a half dozen pistols before he'd gotten three steps. But from the air . . . .

Below him, a crew was refilling the blimp's envelope while others were fueling the tanks. They were preparing to take off. Soon they'd pull back the tarp overhead.

A man dressed in slacks and a pullover sweater stepped into view and spoke to the grey-haired boss. Fowler blinked in surprise. He recognized him immediately: President Franklin Delano Roosevelt. But of course it wasn't. FDR was wheelchair bound from polio. The case was getting stranger every minute.

He had to get word to the Bureau. A radio message would never get through the mesa's stone walls. He'd have to return to the surface for a clear signal. Crouching, Fowler slipped along the catwalk to the stairs. At the landing, he turned to climb the steps and found himself face to face with a pair of men in mechanic's coveralls.

"*Wer bist du?*" the taller one said. Unable to think of a plausible answer, Fowler decked him with a left hook. The shorter one fumbled with a pistol caught in his coverall. He shouted, but it blended with the noise from below and went unnoticed. Fowler head butted him and the mechanic staggered backward onto the catwalk.

The first man had risen to hands and knees and was shaking his head like a wet dog. Fowler rabbit punched him and he went flat on his face. The man on the catwalk had pulled his pistol, a Luger, free of his coverall and snapped off a shot that ricocheted from the red stone inches from Fowler's head.

He fired once and put a round in the gunman's chest. The report, like the shout was unnoticed, but the man staggered backward against the low railing on the catwalk. The agent ran to him, but too late to grab hold before he pitched over and fell into a crowd of men on the floor of the pit.

Fowler took the steps two and three at a time and the thin air caught up with him. He burst through the door at the top into the darkness panting, his lungs on fire. Shouting and footfalls followed close behind. Two silhouettes filled the doorway and Fowler fired, dropping both of them and blocking the opening. He turned and ran blind around the edge of the crater. Behind him, guns erupted and automatic weapon fire sprayed the mesa in random waves. He was on the steep side, but he had no choice. He ran for the edge and sailed off into space.

Like the old saw has it, it's not the fall that kills you, it's the landing. Fowler bounced off the sharp slope and rolled into a boulder that knocked the wind out of him. He'd lost his automatic in the tumble. He fumbled into his jacket and pulled out a small radio transmitter. He put the earpiece in his ear and switched on the battery. The radio howled like a banshee.

Lights appeared over the rim of the mesa. Men were scrambling toward him. He tried to stand and came up at an oblique angle. His head spun and as the spotlights found him, he pitched over unconscious.

Cooper cursed his bad luck. Hobson's choice; he'd chosen the motorcycle nearest the door, and it turned out to be the one with the least fuel in the tank. He was miles from the rendezvous point, and limping on his bad ankle. He'd tried several times to get a message through to his team, but he was still too close to Castle Mesa and his signal was jammed.

He oriented himself by the Pole Star and kept slogging through the sand.

Fowler woke slowly. He cracked one eyelid and saw that he was in a dimly lit room like a cabin on an ocean liner. The round windows showed only blackness. He felt the steady vibration of heavy engines through the couch on which he lay. Fowler took inventory. Slight movement of either leg brought no pain. The same with his arms. He took a deep breath and felt as if he'd been stabbed. He jerked involuntarily. Broken ribs. He was lucky none had punctured a lung.

"He's awake," someone said. A mechanical voice replied, "I'll be there shortly." Fowler tried to place the accent. German? Austrian?

In a moment a door slid open and two men entered the cabin. One was the grey haired boss he'd seen earlier; the other was a man whose bulk filled the doorway, height and width. His face was a mass of the kind of scar tissue that comes from torture, not accident or combat. Whimsical shapes dotted his cheeks and forehead, as if a child were playing with an angry pink crayon. What looked like a man's signature spanned the boulder of a forehead, an artist signing his work with a scalpel. His nose was unnaturally sharp because a wedge had been carved from it and the gap crudely stitched back together.

"Good evening, Agent Fowler." The grey haired man said. "Welcome aboard the Loki. My name is Kurt Volker." He pronounced his first name "court." "My rather large friend is Metz." Definitely Austrian. He brought his face close and Fowler saw the palest blue eyes he could imagine. Definitely Aryan. He turned Fowler's shield over in his fingers. "There is no need to deny your identity. We know who you are and what you are."

"And why I'm here?" Fowler said. He tried to sit up, but found his waist was tied to the bunk.

"You are just another policeman solving a crime; better than most, but still just another policeman."

"That's how it began, but of course there's more to it, isn't there?"

Volker smiled. "Yes, there is. I am sure you have questions, and I am happy to answer them, since you will not live to share the information."

"You're going to kidnap the President when he comes to Topeka tomorrow. Posing as a newsreel blimp, you'll fly over the motorcade and snatch his car off the street like you did the armored van."

"Perhaps I underestimated you, Agent Fowler" Volker said. "Go on."

"And the FDR lookalike—"

"Johann Strauss, one of Munich's finest actors."

"You're going to switch him with Roosevelt."

The smile broadened. Volker nodded. "Yes. There is war coming to Europe, and everything must be done to keep the United States from interfering in our business. We must ensure that your President and your nation remain neutral as long as possible. We will make ransom demands and when they are met, Strauss will take Roosevelt's place."

"'We' meaning Germany, I take it. So you switch your man with the President and he keeps our nose out of the conflict."

"I am glad that was you who stumbled onto us, Agent Fowler. You have the intelligence and the imagination to appreciate what we are doing."

"But surely somebody will figure it out. Sooner or later, someone will know he's not the genuine item."

"It will take long enough for those gears to turn. By the time Strauss is discovered, it will be too late."

"Okay, I get it, but of all the armored shipments to steal, why eighty-two grand in half dollars?"

Volker's eyes gleamed with amusement. "We'll let that be a surprise."

"How did you get this ship here? I know you didn't fly it in. You would have been seen every five minutes."

"Your Customs operation is as corrupt as the rest of your government. The envelope was the most difficult item to smuggle in through Canada. It came in sections disguised as circus tents. The engines are your own Pratt and Whitney manufacture. This oversized gondola was constructed here, as was much of the ship."

"So this operation has been underway for a long time."

"It has been my life for over a year, Agent Fowler. That is why I cannot allow you to interfere with it."

"It's not going to work. You know that. You'll be caught."

"Perhaps, but one must make the attempt."

"My partner saw this oversized gas bag too. He'll report it."

Volker shrugged. "There was an airship. Where is it now? Which way did it fly? By the time your people discover those answers, the deed will be done."

"You can't just fly away. You'll be seen, pursued."

"We have airplanes waiting and automobiles at a sufficient distance. We will ground the Loki and scatter. Your authorities will find an empty vessel.

"What if things go wrong? What if Roosevelt is killed in the attempt? A stray bullet is all it would take."

"Then your Vice-President, 'Cactus Jack' your people call him, would succeed Roosevelt. What is it he said? The vice-presidency is not worth, in his words, 'a bucket of warm piss.' He would be very busy for a long time domestically before he could turn his eyes to international affairs."

"Then why not just assassinate Roosevelt?"

"Because death is permanent. National outrage would be as great in either case, but the nation's relief at their leader's return would calm them for the moment. Volker smiled. "You are very insightful, Agent Fowler. I regret that we do not have the time to play a game of chess. I suspect that you would be a worthy opponent."

He leaned forward and pinned Fowler's badge to his chest. "I appreciate your insightful questions. I have answered them, and now, Agent Fowler, you will tell me what I need to know."

"The hell I will. You can torture me all day. I won't talk."

"I could turn a handsome face like yours into a grotesque mask like Metz's very quickly, but there is no need. Our drugs are more efficient and much less messy. Karl." Volker nodded to the man who had been watching Fowler. He stepped into Fowler's line of sight with a hypodermic needle in his hand.

Fowler struggled, but Metz held him down as if he were a child. A sharp pinch from the needle and in a moment, his conscious will gently floated away like a fallen leaf on a pond.

The team, led by Cooper, a crutch in his armpit, surrounded the mesa by dawn. A detachment of the Arizona National Guard provided three tanks and mounted artillery plus a hundred troops. "You know this comes dangerously close to violating *posse comitatus*," Travers said.

"Uh-huh," Cooper said, nodding, ignoring the comment. He rubbed his aching eyes, exhausted from his trek in the desert, and the day was just beginning.

Overhead, biplanes circled the mesa. Cooper's handset radio crackled. "There's a big hole in the butte," a voice said, "but there's no airship."

"Damn," Cooper said. "The blimp's gone."

Travers turned to the National Guard commander. "Move in."

The raid was an anticlimax. All that remained inside the mesa was a scattering of equipment, two empty fuel tankers, and the painted canvas that hung like a curtain over the west wall of the hollow. No airship. No people. No Fowler.

"I want every inch of this place and the surrounding area searched," Travers said. The soldiers and agents fanned out and went to work. Like ants on an anthill the men combed over the inside and outside of the mesa looking for any trace of Fowler.

In less than an hour, one of the agents found Fowler's automatic where it had slid down the steep side of the mesa.

"He's not here," Cooper said. "I'm keeping my fingers crossed that he's still alive. And if he is, you can bet he's on the case trying to find a way to stop these thugs."

Travers turned to Cooper. "Send the planes out to search for the airship. Something that big can't hide in the sky. Damn it! We need to find Fowler."

Fowler woke with a nasty headache, as if someone were pounding a spike into his skull every time his heart beat. He was tied with heavy twine to a chair in what was apparently the airship's bridge with a view through the front windshield of blue sky over a ceiling of clouds. The sun was just clearing the horizon. They were flying east. Volker stood at the bridge while one of his crew manned the helm.

"Ah, you are awake, Agent Fowler." Volker smiled. "You have—what do you Americans call it? The best seat in the house. Yes."

The face of the gondola was floor to ceiling windows and through the lower ones; Fowler could see an unbroken expanse of cottony clouds. His sense of time was disrupted by the drug. His eyes searched the cabin but found no clock. He twisted his wrist to push his watch out of his cuff but he was bound too tightly to the arms of the seat.

Volker leaned over him and pushed back the sleeve of his shirt for him, exposing the watch, a Bulova Excellency on a segmented stainless steel bracelet. The dial read 8:35. "An interesting timepiece, but flawed." Volker turned his wrist to show a *Glasshütte* chronometer on a leather strap. Its dial read 8:37.

"You should have bought a good German watch, Agent Fowler. Yours is two minutes slow."

"Or yours is two minutes fast," Fowler said, "sending you in before it should."

"No matter," Volker said. "In a few hours, you will see the flawless execution of a flawless plan. Enjoy the show."

Not if I can help it, Fowler thought. He stared at the second hand of his watch as it ticked around the face in an inexorable path. Each second inching toward failure.

One of the flight crew spoke to Volker in German. Fowler caught most of it: "The ceiling is low; we can stay above or in the clouds for most if not all of the journey."

"*Das is gut,*" Volker replied. "*Sehr gut.*" He turned to Fowler. "So, you see, Agent Fowler, the gods are smiling on us this day."

Strauss stepped into Fowler's line of vision. The resemblance was remarkable. Had he not known the man beside him was an impostor, Fowler would not at first glance known that this was not the President. With him was the bald man in his black suit. His head was hairless, and his scalp shone like polished ivory, but not shaved. As he had no hair, neither did he have eyebrows, beard, or mustache. *Alopecia totalis*, Fowler thought. His cold eyes stared at Fowler with unbridled contempt. "This is the FBI Agent?"

"Yes," Volker said. "Agent Daniel Fowler, meet Herr Mueller. As you can see, Herr Mueller, he is no threat to our operation."

"But he is only one," Mueller snapped in German. "Your men found two parachutes. You let the other escape. Half is not good enough." Mueller emphasized the words "you," and "half." His tone was like slapping Volker across the face. Behind Mueller, Metz bridled, clenching his fists, and Fowler thought for a moment that the giant would twist the German's bald head from his neck. A quick jerk of Volker's head warned Metz away

"There is no need for concern, Herr Mueller. In a few hours, we will be over our target. Apart from this minor intrusion, things have gone as planned in every detail. We found the motorcycle his partner stole a few miles from the mesa out of fuel. "We didn't find him, but we lifted off on schedule, so he could not have informed his superiors in time to interfere. There has been no damage."

"For your sake, I hope you are right." Mueller leaned forward to lock eyes with Fowler. "FBI," Mueller said in precise English. "Foolish Bastards Indeed." He sneered as he said it, and as he did, Fowler spat in the hairless face.

Rather than react, Mueller stood impassive for a moment. He wiped his face with a handkerchief then reached into his pocket for a switchblade knife. He

"You should have bought a good German watch."

pressed the button, and five inches of shining steel swung out with a loud click.

"I would enjoy killing you now, Agent Fowler," Mueller said in English, "but I want you to witness your failure before Metz throws you out of this gondola. I want you to think about that failure all the way to the ground. Metz! Hold him."

Huge hands clamped around Fowler's head and held it immobile.

Mueller put the tip of the knife on the bridge of Fowler's nose. "But you need only one eye to see it. Shall I take the left or the right? Which do you prefer?"

"Herr Volker!" The helmsman shouted. "An airplane!"

Everyone turned to follow the helmsman's pointing finger. A bright yellow biplane paralleled the blimp to its left.

"I thought no airplane could fly as high as this craft," Mueller snarled at Volker, turning away from Fowler. "That's twice you've erred, Volker. Perhaps I should take your eye instead."

The yellow plane tipped its wings in greeting then swooped under the gondola to pop up on the right. The plane had the standard NC numbers on its tail. The pilot waved, He wore a leather helmet with goggles, and so did his passenger, whose long, dark hair streamed out behind her. A woman. The couple were out on a jaunt, enjoying the adventure.

"It appears to be a civilian craft," the helmsman said.

Mueller turned to Volker. "No matter. They have seen us. Shoot them down."

Volker hesitated but knew better than to argue. He nodded to Metz who left the bridge.

Go away, Fowler thought. *Get out of here.*

The biplane did a barrel roll. *Dear God,* Fowler thought. *The pilot saw the Castle News logo on the side of the blimp and he thinks they'll film him if he shows off.*

The pilot tipped his wings to the left, then to the right, exposing the belly of the craft. From the deck above, a machine gun chattered and stitched a line of holes through the fuselage. Black smoke poured from the engine, and the plane veered sharply into a tailspin, disappearing through the clouds below.

Mueller folded his knife. "I've decided that we'll conclude our personal business later, Agent Fowler. I'll leave you wonder when that will occur." Mueller turned to Volker. "And we will discuss your shortcomings later as well, Volker." Mueller turned on his heel and strode off the bridge.

"The arrogant bastard. I could kill him right now," Metz snarled under his breath.

"As could I, Metz, but some things are more important than personal satisfaction."

The National Guard commander, a Captain named Ellison called Travers and Cooper over. Two soldiers were standing beside him. "My men have found something." He gestured to the truck parked nearby. "Let's take a ride."

A little less than a mile away from the mesa, Cooper saw a handful of uniforms standing with two of his agents. The soldiers snapped to attention when Ellison climbed out of the truck. A sergeant said, "We didn't know what to make of this, sir. We found a patch of these in the sand." He held out his hand, and in his palm was a shiny new half dollar.

"How many of these did you find?" Travers said.

"Nobody counted them yet. As soon as the Guardsmen found the first few, we cordoned off the area to keep from mucking up the scene, but it looks as if there are at least a hundred."

They looked across the sand and saw a scatter of coins sparkling in the rising sun.

The sergeant went on. "There were no tracks anywhere around. It was as if they just fell out of the sky."

"They probably did," Cooper said.

"What do you think?" Travers asked. "Did the coins fall out of the van while they were flying over?"

Cooper raised his eyes to the clouds. "That, or it was deliberate."

"That makes no sense," Ellison said. "Why go to the trouble of stealing money then throwing it away?"

"I'm afraid we're going to find out before much longer."

The blimp glided over the clouds and the monotony of the view aggravated Fowler's sense of anger and futility. Volker found him in the way on the bridge, so he had Metz remove him to the cabin where he first woke. Metz simply lifted Fowler chair and all and carried him down the corridor. He set the chair in the middle of the cabin and left, closing the door and locking it.

The scheme was insane but ingenious at the same time. What chilled Fowler was the thought that the men putting it in motion were not. They were cold, calculating, and methodical. Fowler doubted the plan would succeed, but the threat to the President was real, not to mention the danger to the crowd that would gather along the motorcade route. Fowler imagined the big Packard touring car dangling from a chain, Secret Service agents hanging desperately from the running boards, and the President helpless in the back seat.

Fowler had to do something. He tried his bonds one at a time. Both wrists were lashed firmly to the arms of the chair. A rope wound around his waist and the chair back, and his ankles were secured to its legs. If he'd been awake, Fowler might have tried Houdini's trick of tensing his muscles as the twine was tied then letting them relax, allowing a little slack, but that was not an option. He imagined Volker's men, or perhaps Metz tugging at the knots with all their strength, making him one with the chair.

Fowler's right leg allowed a little movement up and down. If he could work the rope off the chair leg, he could free his foot. If he could free one, he could free the other. It was a start.

He began moving his knee up and down, an inch or so at first. The rough hemp rope painfully abraded his skin through his trousers, and soon his sock was wet from blood, but the blood lubricated the rope and the chair leg. The rope began to move, barely at first, but Fowler could feel it gradually slipping down. He shifted his thigh to push at an angle, and in a moment, the rope slipped off the end of the chair leg.

He raised his leg to cross it over his knee so that he could twist off the hollow heel of his shoe and get to the flexible strip of steel hidden in the shank, razor edged on one side, serrated like a hacksaw blade on the other. He twisted his hand as far as it could reach and found that the blade could reach the rope at his wrist. Fowler opted for the saw edge, and soon, the hemp fibers began to fray.

His hand cramped in the unnatural position, and more than once Dan had to stop to get it working again. On the third round, the blade cut through. The twine popped, and he could work his hand free. In a moment, he cut the twine from his other hand and foot. Fowler stood carefully, feeling the needles as his circulation returned. Outside the porthole, he no longer saw blue sky. Instead, he saw only uniform whiteness. He felt his ears pop. They were descending.

The lock clicked, and the cabin door slid open. Karl backed into the room carrying a tray with another needle and vial. His head turned and he saw the empty chair. Before he could cry out, Fowler clubbed him from behind and he went to his knees. The tray clattered to the floor, the syringe rolling one way and the vial another. Another rabbit punch, and the crewman was out.

Fowler searched him and was disappointed that Karl carried no gun. But if nothing else, the syringe might be weapon enough. He filled it from the vial. He opened the cabin door an inch. No one in sight, but there were voices down the corridor. He looked out the porthole. The clouds were above the airship now, and he could see land below.

If he could find the radio room, he might get a message off to the Bureau, or to anyone who might alert the Secret Service. A quick search of the cabin yielded nothing useful. He still had his cutting tool and the syringe. His wits would have to make up the difference. Karl's tunic was a bad fit, but it would make Fowler less conspicuous. He donned Karl's cap, slid the door open, and slipped into the corridor.

Cooper drove to the airfield with a handful of agents. Over three hundred days of sunshine every year in Denver, and today had to be overcast, making the blimp a huge needle in a giant grey haystack. If they found the blimp, it would be sheer luck at this point.

The search team was assembled in a hangar when Cooper arrived. He was halfway through his briefing when a soldier came in with a note. "This just came in, Agent."

Cooper read it quickly. "We just received a report that a private plane went down outside Russell, Kansas, the pilot and passenger are dead. Police on the scene thought it was an ordinary crash til they saw the bullet holes in the fuselage. It was shot down. Now we have a direction."

Murmurs arose from the team.

"These boys play for keeps. If you spot the blimp, do not engage with it. Radio it in and keep your distance. We'll follow up with the Shrikes. In the meantime, we'll put out the word a hundred miles east to be on the watch."

"You'll be flying with us?" one of the pilots said.

Cooper nodded. "Don't worry about me, I'm combat trained. My partner's out there, dead or alive. I wouldn't miss it for anybody's money."

Fowler crept down the passageway. There was literally no place to hide in it. The first door he tried was locked. The second opened into a storage room. He ducked in it to hide for a moment and to take stock of his injuries. The broken ribs were painful, but he was able to tape them up with a roll of adhesive tape from a medical kit he found bolted to the wall.

His sense of balance was a little shaky from the residual effect of the drugs he'd been given, that and the thin air. He had no way of knowing their exact altitude, but being in the clouds was indication enough that they were flying in the five digits, probably hiding their passage by gliding in the white froth, unseen from the ground to their destination.

A loudspeaker crackled, and Fowler heard Volker's voice say, *"Alle Stationen: zehn minuten bis zum Ziel."* All stations: ten minutes to target. That explained the empty corridor. Volker's crew was in the lower level preparing for the operation.

Fowler found a cabin with its door ajar. He peered through the opening to see Johann Strauss sitting before a mirror. He was dressed in casual clothing, presumably to change into Roosevelt's suit once the abduction took place. The actor was consulting a photograph of the President, and tilting his head one way and the other, trying to copy the exact angle of FDR's chin and the degree of his eyelids' closure. "My fellow Americans," Strauss said; once, twice, several times, rehearsing the precise inflection of the President's speech. Dan slid the door open and stepped into the cabin.

Strauss saw Fowler in the mirror, and his eyes went wide with surprise. He turned in the chair, and Fowler punched him in the jaw, knocking him from his chair to the deck. One punch was enough. Strauss didn't move.

If I can't stop this plot from the beginning, I'll stop it from the other end, Fowler thought, and used his blade to carve the word FAKE into Strauss' forehead. Blood welled out to form angry red letters. There would be no switch. Now it was up to him to keep the President from harm at any cost.

Fifteen thousand people lined up over a two mile course along Kansas Street, a main thorofare of Topeka. That was the estimate of the local police as to how many people would turn out for the parade. The threat of rain did little to deter the throngs of people craning their necks to enjoy the pomp and circumstance.

Some were well-dressed, but most wore shabby clothes, and looked as if they'd come from a bread line. Prosperity may be making a comeback somewhere, but not in Kansas, where the land literally blew away from the Dust Bowl. These people had come to see the President and to see for themselves that someone cared enough about their plight to come and offer hope. On their faces was a mix of stoicism and desperation. School children were gathered near the end of the parade, each given a small penny flag on a stick to wave when FDR passed by. The money would be better spent to feed them, Edwin Miller, chief of the Secret Service detail thought, but diversion should brighten their lives, at least for a day. And the adults—Juvenal was right: "Give them bread and circuses, and they will never revolt."

Miller scanned the layout of the motorcade. The Presidential limousine, an oversized Packard touring car, its suspension jacked up to make FDR more visible was surrounded by almost two dozen motorcycle patrolman, gloved, helmeted, and uniformed, making an impressive display of security. A carload of agents, armed with heavy weaponry, would ride ten feet behind the Packard.

Plain-clothes agents would march alongside the car and behind it, watching the crowd, ready in case some lunatic might break out and rush the Packard. Fifteen thousand people. Any random loon might harbor a grudge against FDR, his politics, or his policies. One nut, they could handle, but Miller had nightmares about an entire crowd suddenly going berserk and like the Red Sea closing on the Pharaoh to swarm over the Packard and tear its passenger apart. His men couldn't fire fast enough, and there simply weren't enough bullets on hand.

Two of his men were helping the President from his wheelchair into the back of the limousine. Boarding a second car were incumbent Democratic Senator, George McGill, and Governor Walter Augustus Huxman, Alf Landon's successor. Republican Senator Arthur Capper declined the invitation.

Overhead, in the overcast sky, Miller saw the bulk of an airship, a blimp, a dirigible—he never really understood the difference between the two. Banner Aerial News was cleared to film newsreel footage that would run in every movie theater in the country, reassuring Americans that their President was on the job, and so were his Democratic cronies.

He'd be happy to see this event over and done, a two-mile ride ending at the

Capitol on Van Buren for speeches and a reception geared to bolster McGill's sagging chances for re-election. Miller hated politics, but he had a job to do, and he did it without flinching.

One of his men signaled from the limousine. The President's car was ready. Miller held up three fingers. The sooner this ride was over, the happier he'd be.

Fowler climbed down the ladder to the lower tier of the Loki's gondola, which was a large open space crowded with the blimp's engines and other machinery, gears and pulleys. The crewmen were attentive to their tasks, and no one noticed him at first. He picked up a coil of rope and shouldered it to hide his face and moved toward a porthole.

His ears popped again and as he looked outside, the blimp broke out of the clouds and he saw a city below.

Topeka.

At the fore end of the gondola Fowler saw light as a bay opened and a hopper was wheeled to its edge by a half dozen crewmen, Metz with them. It was filled with shiny half dollars.

On the bridge, Volker and Mueller were watching the city below them. In a few moments, a year's worth of planning and work would come to fruition.

A crewman burst into the bridge. "Herr Volker!" He shouted. "The American has escaped."

Volker almost laughed. *Escaped? To where?* "We are about to execute our operation, Gustav. There is nothing he can do to stop it. He can go nowhere. We will find him later."

"But, sir, he has disfigured Strauss."

Mueller's head whipped around. The look in his eyes told Volker his future was in jeopardy. "You will find him now."

Below, the motorcade began to move. Miller stood on the running board of the Packard with one of his men while two others rode the other side. The local VFW band struck up "The Stars and Stripes Forever" as they marched in the lead. Ahead, Miller saw the corridor of buildings, most no more than four stories tall, but a few, like the ornate Kansas Capitol Building and Loan Bank towered seven stories or more.

An agent ran to the side of the car. Miller couldn't hear what he said over the rumble of the motorcycle escort, the cheering of the crowd, and the brassy blare of the band. He pointed frantically upward. Overhead, a second airship hovered above the limousine.

Miller's instinct kicked in. He clambered into the front seat and shouted into the driver's ear, "Get us out of here! I'll have the escort clear a path at the next intersection!" He jumped to the street and ran toward the lead motor-cycle, but not quite fast enough.

As he ran, Miller felt something hit him on the head, then another hit his shoulder. It rolled across the pavement into the crowd. He stopped and stared. It was a shiny half dollar. Suddenly it was raining money, coins bouncing off the street, the sidewalk, the limousine, and the helmets of the motorcycle cops.

The crowd saw it too. A man in tattered clothes pointed and shouted, "Look! Money!" and in seconds, they pushed aside the saw horse barricades and swarmed into the street from all directions, scooping up the coins. The police and the Secret Service agents tried first to hold them back, then real-izing the futility, circled the Packard and the Governor's car as the frenzied crowd climbed over each other and trampled each other underfoot in the rush to grab at the silver bonanza.

The limousine driver edged the Packard forward, blowing the horn, nudg-ing people out of the way and trying to make it the half block to the intersec-tion. One of the agents threw the President to the floor of the car and lay over him as cover.

Miller looked up the street. Word had spread. The cheering crowd had become a wild-eyed mob running from all directions. The motorcycle detail had dismounted and were swinging their Billy clubs two- handed, beating the rioters down, but more kept coming. They began climbing onto the fend-ers and running boards of the Packard to grab at the coins that lay on the car.

Miller drew his pistol and was about to give the order to fire into the crowd when the scene took another bizarre twist. The belly of the Loki's gondola opened like a two-leaved trapdoor, and a heavy motor thrummed into action. Steel jaws like steam shovel buckets lowered on heavy chains heading for the limousine.

The men in the gondola were too intent on their roles and watching the scene below to notice Fowler up to now, but that was about to change. He stepped up beside the winch operator and clubbed the side of his head with an elbow. The operator went over sideways. Which lever? He was reaching for the first one when a crewmen grabbed him from behind, an arm around Fowler's throat.

He drove an elbow into his attacker's gut, and when his grip slackened, Fowler threw him over his shoulder. The crewman rolled toward the edge of the trapdoor. He grabbed frantically for anything to stop himself, but he went over the edge, his scream unheard in the rumble of the machinery.

Fowler looked up to see Metz circling around the machinery, a look of pure fury on his scarred face.

Cooper led the trio of airplanes. They followed the line from the mesa over the crash site and moved forward, hoping to get a glimpse of the blimp. He keyed his radio and asked the other pilots, what's the city up ahead? Over."

The radio crackled. "Topeka," came the reply.

Copper thought, *Topeka. Where did I hear about Topeka?* Then he remembered.

The radio crackled again. "I see it!" one of the pilots said. "Ten o'clock. Wait! There's two of them!"

Fowler was cornered. Metz was going to kill him, so he decided to cause as much trouble as he could on his way out. He grabbed a spanner and threw it into the gears of the winch. They stopped turning, but the powerful motor continued to grind at the wrench, bending the steel like taffy.

Metz reached for Fowler, and the agent's foot lashed out with a kick to the giant's knee. Metz roared in pain but kept coming. His arms wrapped around Fowler's waist and he lifted him off the deck. The pain in Fowler's ribs was horrific, and it was his turn to shout. Dan beat at Metz's face with his fists, but it made no difference.

Metz squeezed harder. Another moment, and he would snap Fowler's spine.

Dan pulled the syringe from his pocket and drove it into Metz's neck. He thumbed the plunger and emptied the syringe into Metz's carotid artery, the expressway to his brain. Metz seemed unaffected for a good two seconds, then his eyes rolled back in his head, and he lost his grip on Fowler, who fell to the deck.

Metz staggered backwards, lost his footing, and fell into the gears of the winch. At that moment, the pressure on the wrench became too great. It snapped in two, and the winch began to lower the jaws again. The gears grabbed at the giant's jacket, and pulled him head first into the mechanism. Blood and brains sprayed the gears, and they kept turning, unaffected.

The other crewmen saw the fight and two of them were coming for him, one drawing a pistol. Fowler made a quick decision and jumped through the open bay. He caught one of the chains and afraid to look down, began scrambling hand over hand to the bottom.

A rioter climbed onto the running board of the Packard and Miller clubbed him with his automatic. He fell backward and disappeared into the mass of bodies to be trampled by the frenzied mob.

The driver continued the crawl, the heavy limousine pushing the crowd ahead of him. He held down the horn button. Even if he floored the gas pedal and knocked the first fifty of the rioters flat, there was no guarantee the car wouldn't be hung up on the pile of bodies. The mob had descended into complete madness, behaving with wild abandon, fighting over the coins on the ground, and fighting to wrest them from each other. Miller saw one woman clutching a handful of silver to her breast try to escape to the sidewalk. A man grabbed at the coins and she struggled until he head butted her and the coins fell into the forest of legs, lost to them both. She stood screaming, her face a bloody mask as people swirled around her like hornets.

A bald man in overalls, his hat lost in the scuffle, crammed a handful of silver into his mouth and tried to back away from the fight. But he was seen, and a tall man clamped his hands around the farmer's throat and shook him like a rag doll until he spat out the coins to be lost underfoot.

Three men grabbed the driver and dragged him from his seat. As soon as his foot left the clutch, the Packard bucked and stalled. The crush of bodies closed on the car, and Miller knew they were trapped. All that was left him was to save the President. He raised his hand to signal his men to open fire and stopped when he looked up. Miller saw the steel jaws slowly lowering on chains from the belly of the blimp overhead, that and something else, a man climbing down the heavy links. What the hell was going on?

Overhead, Volker had run to the gondola's hold. A crewman shouted, "Metz is dead. The American escaped. He's climbing down the chain."

Volker manned the controls. Damn that Fowler, he thought, then put the agent out of his mind. He had to make the mission succeed in spite of him. He spoke into the intercom, "Bridge, hold our position, be ready to rise on my signal." He reached for the lever that would close the jaws.

The links were the size one might find on an ocean liner's anchor chain, and Fowler was able to work quickly to the steel jaws. It was only about fifty feet, but it felt like climbing down the face of the Grand Canyon. Worse, the jaws swung side to side. He finally had the nerve to look down and saw the chaos in the street. The limousine was only ten feet below. A man in a suit was aiming an automatic at him. Fowler let go of the chain and hoped he'd land on something soft.

He dropped into the broad back seat of the Packard, knocking Miller off his feet. Miller was about to shoot when he saw Fowler's badge.

"FBI! FBI!" Fowler shouted. "We have to get the President out." He jerked his thumb upward. "They're going to snatch the car!"

Miller saw the steel jaws closing and didn't argue. The scene couldn't get any crazier. "Okay!" he shouted. "Get out of the car!" Fowler jumped from the running board as the jaws crushed the sides of the Packard inward with a screech of tortured metal. The car shuddered, and slowly rose from the pavement.

Miller yanked a side panel from the rear door of the limousine exposing a lever. He tugged at it, and a section of the floor dropped on hinges, making a ramp to the street level. The President and the agent on top of him rolled onto the pavement, shielded by the car.

"Come on !" Miller shouted, jumping to the pavement. Fowler and Miller dragged the President from beneath the car. Miller and the other agent heaved him over Fowler's shoulder and fought to clear the way through the melee to safety.

The street looked like chaos personified from the air, but in the middle of it, the riot looked even worse to Fowler. He had read of the mob mentality, the abandonment of moral obedience to an anonymous, collective frenzy. Here it was all around him.

The fight was no longer over a few coins on the street. It had become a pitched battle between the mob and the police, and its members with each other. Complete insanity had taken over. Fowler saw one of the rioters beating a helmeted cop with his own nightstick. A second man took his pistol from the holster. He stood up and spun around wildly, looking for a target. Miller saw it too and fired.

The rioter went down, but his companion dropped the nightstick, scooped up the revolver, and fired back. One second Miller was beside Fowler fighting through the crowd; the next, he was down.

Those shots changed the face of the rioters from fury to panic. Suddenly, everyone in the street wanted out, and collided with the crush of people wanting in. Fowler stepped over bodies, some living, and some not. He looked over his shoulder. The Packard was five feet off the ground and rising.

Cooper wasn't sure which airship was the enemy at first. He buzzed the one that said Banner Aerial News, and the cameramen waved to him. He circled around toward the Castle News blimp and saw the Packard dangling like a rabbit in the claws of an eagle.

Fowler and Miller dragged the President from beneath the car.

He circled again, and this time saw bright muzzle flashes from the gondola. They were shooting machine guns at him.

Time to shoot back.

Cooper knew the blimp's envelope wouldn't pop like a kid's balloon and crash it into the streets below, but enough holes in the gas bag would keep it from reaching full altitude and hiding in the clouds again. He raked the blimp with fire from the Shrike's four machine guns mounted in the wheel fairings. The other two planes followed his lead, swooping around the airship like their namesake harrying a crow.

The next pass, Cooper aimed for the gondola.

On the lower deck, Volker ran the winch, slowly raising the Packard toward the blimp. Things had gone terribly wrong, but fortune favors the brave. The mission could still be saved. Perhaps they could reach the rendezvous twenty miles away. Mueller could still interrogate Roosevelt under the influence of their drugs and pry the nation's secrets from him even if they could not exchange Strauss for him. "Forward!" he shouted into the intercom to the Captain on the bridge. The heavy engines thundered, and the blimp began moving down the street through the corridor of buildings.

The buildings shielded the blimp from the airplanes at first, making the gondola a hard target, but as it rose, the gondola was exposed. Cooper banked right and turned to fly head on into the blimp's path.

The Loki's captain carefully navigated the space as the blimp rose. The street was straight and broad, and posed little trouble for the blimp, but the car, dangling like a fetus from an umbilical cord, swung side to side. It ripped down electrical lines, which fell into the street and into the crowd, then clear of them, caromed off the building facades. "*Sheen!*" cried the navigator. The Captain turned his attention from the buildings to look forward and saw the Shrike flying straight at him.

Then the guns began to fire.

The glass front of the cabin exploded. Shards of glass sprayed the crew and so did the rounds from Cooper's guns. The Captain, struck by the gunfire, fell backward pulling the ship's wheel to starboard. The navigator rushed to the wheel to correct their course, but it was too late. The Loki collided with the seven-story bank building, its ornate terra cotta cornices ripping a gash in the envelope.

On the lower deck, Mueller strode to Volker, oblivious to the frenzy around him. "You will answer for this failure, Volker!" he shouted in German. "I will personally..." He stopped in mid-sentence as Volker turned toward him and he saw the look in Volker's eye.

At that moment, something snapped in Volker's brain. He grabbed Mueller by his lapels and lifted him off the floor. Mueller kicked and screamed as Volker carried him to the open bay doors. He pulled his knife from his pocket and pushed the button. The blade sprang out as Mueller's feet dangled over the opening. Volker looked into his face and said simply, "*Sterben.*" Die.

Mueller stabbed Volker's belly frantically, three, four times, and hit a vital spot. Volker's eyes went blank, and he pitched forward through the hatch, taking Mueller with him.

Fowler reached a narrow walkway between two buildings and found a *cul de sac* away from the riot. He was gasping for air and every breath was a stab in his ribs.

"You can put me down now," his burden said.

Fowler crouched and laid the President as gently as he could on the brick pavement, propping him against the wall of a building.

"Thank you. That was a close call."

To Fowler's amazement, the President stood up. "Let's get further away from here." He took off his suit coat and Fowler saw a holstered automatic in his armpit. "Give me your jacket, the suit's a dead giveaway."

"You're—you're," Fowler stammered.

He held out his hand to shake. "My name is George Hartwell. Pleased to meet you."

"A double?"

Hartwell nodded. "I'm one of three. It's the best kept secret in Washington. They can't risk trucking the real President around."

"The Secret Service—don't they know?"

"Only the boys at the top in D.C. They figured the agents wouldn't be so attentive if they knew I was a fake." Hartwell chuckled. "They're good shots but not good actors. It's all about image."

From the street a block away Fowler heard the diminishing sounds of the riot; shouts, screams, a stray gunshot. All those people, injured, some of them dead, all for a political pageant. His life and others' lives risked to save a goddamned actor. When he punched Hartwell in the mouth, his ribs screamed, but it felt good anyway.

The Loki, despite the rip in the bag, made it miles past the city limits and came to rest in a farmer's field. The few living crewmen leaped from the gondola before it touched down and ran to avoid being covered by the sagging envelope. A burst of fire from the airplanes raised puffs of dust across their path and stopped them cold. They threw down their weapons and threw up their hands.

Fowler went back to the street, which looked like a battlefield. As quickly as it started, the violence suddenly stopped. Dozens of bodies, the living and the dead, littered the pavement. The police had cleared the street. The roar of the crowd was gone, replaced by the cries and moans of the hurt and the dying. Sirens wailed in the distance as ambulances came from every direction.

He found the body of the Secret Service Agent, whose name he later learned was Miller, lying face up, a gunshot wound to his chest. Beside him lay a shining fifty-cent piece spattered with blood.

It was tails.

Fowler wished he had punched Hartwell twice.

Fowler sat in the hallway of Topeka General's Emergency room. The corridor was filled with bodies on cots and gurneys, some with sheets pulled to their chins, and some with sheets pulled over their faces as the staff scurried from patient to patient. Triage was the order of the moment, and hard decisions were made; who would live and who wouldn't, whose condition demanded first attention; who could suffer a while but live to show off their scars.

Since he walked into the Emergency Room under his own steam, Fowler was a Category III, a person with injuries that didn't require ambulance transport. His chest hurt, and he was afraid one of his broken ribs had punctured something important. He'd been there for three hours already, and it looked as if he'd be there for several more.

"Dan?"

He turned to see Coop elbowing his way through the crowded hallway.

"Glad you made it to the party."

"Man, am I glad to see you."

"Did they get away?"

Cooper shook his head. "We got 'em. The blimp went down just outside of town."

"The Loki," Fowler said.

"Huh?"

"The name of the airship. Loki, the trickster in Norse mythology."

"Well, this is one trick that fell flat. Literally. How bad you hurt?"

"A couple of broken ribs, a lot of bumps and bruises, but I'll live."

"I was sent to find you. Travers is here, and he wants a joint debriefing with the Secret Service boys."

Fowler stood and winced at the pain. "I guess that's no worse torture than sitting here for half the day. Let's go." As they stepped outside, an ambulance was unloading bodies and laying them in a neat row on the sidewalk. One of them was Volker, his sweater brown with dried blood. Beside him Mueller lay; his ivory skull split open.

"Who are they?" Cooper said.

"The bad guys." Fowler turned away. "I need a cigarette. And a drink."

The debriefing was held in the Police Chief's office. The police kept the gang of newshounds and photographers on the sidewalk. Their shouted questions at Cooper and Fowler went unanswered as the pair was escorted into the building.

Travers, as the ranking official present, ran the show. When Fowler came in, Travers said, "I need to speak to Agent Fowler alone. Excuse us, please." The room cleared except for Travers, and Fowler took a chair on the other side of the desk from him.

"Good work, Agent Fowler. You saved the President."

"The hell I did!" Fowler snapped. "I saved a phony, a lookalike."

Travers leveled a cold stare at him. "You saved the President. That's the official story, and that's how you'll tell it."

"How can you sit there and expect me to lie through my teeth about this? People were hurt, people were killed."

"We all take our orders from someone, Agent Fowler, and those are ours."

"Did you know he was a phony?"

Travers shook his head. "None of us did. We didn't even know about the Presidential connection til Cooper figured it out. What if it had been the real FDR? Would there have been fewer casualties? I doubt it. The people who perpetrated this insane scheme posed a real and tangible threat to National Security. Swallow your self-righteous indignation and play the hero."

"Who else knows the truth about this?"

"Precious few, Fowler. Precious few, and the truth stays in this room."

The debriefing lasted nearly three hours, the bulk of it Fowler and Cooper laying out the path of the investigation. When it was over, Fowler was exhausted, but before he could sleep, he had to call Sally. A security lid on the operation meant that she would know nothing about the last twenty-four hours or why she hadn't heard from him.

Travers went outside to talk to the reporters and deliver the official version while Fowler and Cooper were taken out the back door of the police station to avoid the Press. In minutes it spread across the networks to blare from every radio in the country: the FBI and the Secret Service foiled a plot by Anarchists to abduct the President of the United States. Details to follow.

But Travers knew as well as Fowler whose plot it really was. Volker and his crew were of no nation, simply tools, hired guns working for Germany, who could disavow any connection to the plot.

Larger gears were turning in the background.

"That was a bitch," Cooper said. "Time to celebrate staying alive."

Fowler nodded. "At least til next time."

The agency secured rooms for Cooper and Fowler in the Hotel Jayhawk, and the pair agreed to meet in an hour for dinner and drinks. Fowler said he wanted to get cleaned up, but what he really wanted was to call Sally Vane.

When he closed the door to his room, Fowler was stunned by the sudden silence; the absence of chaos was sweet. A new set of clothes hung in the closet, with a note that Fowler's belongings would be delivered from the Denver office the next day. Of course, Dan thought. They want me to look good for the photographers.

He sat on the bed and picked up the telephone. It was six in the evening, seven in D.C. Sally should be at home. He gave the operator the number and after a few clicks and buzzes, heard the ring halfway across the country. Three rings, four. He let it ring twelve times before he hung up.

Fowler's next call was to the Bureau's headquarters. He identified himself to the operator and asked to speak to Agent Vane. She answered on the first ring.

"Sally?"

"Dan," she said, and began to sob.

"I'm okay, Sally."

There was silence for a moment as she composed herself.

"I called your apartment, but you weren't there."

"We've all been called in because of the attempt on the President. We're on high alert. The Bureau's afraid it may be part of something bigger. Where are you?"

Fowler took a long breath before he answered. What to tell Sally, and how much? Who might be listening on the phone? "Topeka. That's all I can say. That and I'm a little worse for wear, but I'm all right."

"The rumor was you were there, in the middle of the riot and the attempt on the President, but no one would confirm anything. Not even whether you were alive or . . . ." Sally's sentence went unfinished. She understood that Dan's words meant high security and didn't press him further.

"It'll be all over the papers in the morning," Dan said. *All over the papers*, he thought, *but not all of the story.*

They made small talk for a few minutes and Dan said, "I should be back in

D.C. in a day or two."

"I'd come out there right now, but I can't get away."

"I know. It's all right, Sally." Fowler sighed. "We'll be together again soon."

He hung up the phone and stared at the wall. Sally's voice was a comfort, but as soon as it was gone, he felt worse than before he called her. He rang Cooper's room and canceled their dinner plans. Then he called room service to order a rare steak and a bottle. When it arrived, he hung the Do not Disturb sign on the doorknob.

Eighteen hours later, Fowler climbed out of a taxi in front of the Justice Department Building. D.C. looked the same as ever, bustling with the business of government, business as usual as if the day before hadn't even happened. The cabbie who drove him from Washington-Hoover Airport recognized him from his picture on the front page of the *Post*, and asked him to autograph the article: Heroic Agent Saves President.

Fowler scanned it as he rode into the center of the city. It was the official story, short on details, with more promised to follow. The account made him out to be a cross between Doc Savage and Secret Agent X. FDR was quoted as saying, "I am grateful, and the Nation is grateful to Agent Fowler for his bravery and resourcefulness. Let this be a reminder to our adversaries that it takes only one good American to thwart the schemes of all their hands."

Fowler wanted to crumple the page in his fist and throw it out the window, but out of consideration to the driver, he signed the page under his official Bureau photograph. Beside it was a photo of the Loki, the Presidential limousine dangling from its chains. The title of the article below the fold read: Fourteen Dead, Dozens Injured in Topeka Riot.

When he got out of the taxi, he asked what fare he owed. The cabbie said, "Nothin', Mister Fowler. It's been an honor to have you in my cab." As he drove away, Dan's face reddened, half with embarrassment and half with anger.

He would have taken the stairs as he usually did, but his aching ribs said "not today."

Marty, the elevator operator said as he got on, "Morning, Agent Fowler. Thank you for a job well done." When he stepped out on his floor, everyone in sight stopped what they were doing and burst into spontaneous applause. They gathered around him, patting his back, pumping his hand and congratulating him.

Down the corridor, Sally stepped out of an office holding a half-dozen files. She dropped them on the floor and ran to him, pushing her way through the well-wishers to throw her arms around him, not caring who saw it or what they might think.

"Oh, Dan," she sobbed. She squeezed him and he gasped with the pain, but at the moment he didn't really mind.

Ellis Stone appeared at the fringe of the group. "Agent Fowler," he said.

"Don't tell me. The Director wants me."

Stone nodded. They said in unison, "Now."

As they walked toward the Director's office, Stone handed him a handkerchief. "You might want to wipe the lipstick off the corner of your mouth."

"No need. This will be a short meeting."

The Director sat at his desk. Newspapers were spread in front of him. "Please sit down, Agent Fowler."

Fowler sat in one of the Inquisition chairs. He stared across the desk at the Director, who turned the *New York Times* around so that Fowler could read yet another congratulatory headline. "I appreciate your comment about teamwork and sharing credit."

"I said what Regional Director Travers told me to say." Missing from the sentence was the word "sir."

"You will receive a commendation for your work on this case, and the President would like to have you come to the White House to thank you personally."

"For what?" Fowler snapped. "For saving some actor?"

Fowler's outburst was met with an impassive stare, as if he hadn't spoken. "You performed an important service to your country yesterday, Agent Fowler, and it should not go unrecognized."

"I'm sure the press will be there too. It's all just a show anyway."

"A necessary show, Agent Fowler. An attempt was made to abduct the President. America is very fragile now, and the people need to see that their confidence in its institutions, including ourselves, is not misplaced."

The Director folded his hands, one over the other. "It is an unfortunate part of our job, and everyone else's in this administration, to nurture that confidence. At times, the truth is a casualty."

Fowler's nostrils flared. "Let me tell you about casualties. People died! People were hurt! And for what? For a circus parade to prop up the re-election chances of some hack politician. And the whole thing was a fake!"

"And if it had been the real Roosevelt? What would be different today, except for your sense of self-righteousness?"

Fowler's face flushed.

"Foreign agents perpetrated a heinous plot on our soil. We stopped it. You stopped it. That is what matters. What if they had succeeded? The ruse wouldn't have lasted long, but the wound to the people's confidence would have been grievous; to think that we can't protect our leader in the center of America's heartland.

"This country is tiptoeing on a tightrope, Agent Fowler. People are behaving themselves because they believe we're on track. They have hope that our way of life is returning. Shake that tightrope, make us flap our arms, look like we have lost our balance, and watch what happens. You saw firsthand how quickly docile people became savages, how years of desperation and poverty broke through the crust of civility and compliance. Had you not succeeded, that riot in Topeka would be piddling small compared to the chaos that might come next.

"The American people need to believe, and we have to protect that belief as surely as we have to protect our leaders. The people desperately need a hero, and this incident has given them one….you."

Fowler stood. "That's a great speech." Something landed on the pile of newspapers. It was a bloody half-dollar. "Give that to Roosevelt for me. Tell the White House they can find a double for me too to smile for the cameras." His badge landed beside the bloody coin.

The Director looked Fowler in the eye and said, "This is no isolated incident. War is coming again to Europe, and it won't leave us unaffected. We will stand by our allies, and Germany knows it. They will weaken us any way they can. We have to fight them here before we have to fight them there. Your country needs men like you to beat these sons of bitches, Dan. The Bureau needs you. I need you."

Neither spoke for a full minute. They stared at each other like gunfighters, each waiting for the other to make a move.

Fowler picked up his shield. He held it in his palm for a moment, staring at it as if he were seeing it for the first time. His eyes locked with the Director's.

"For my country," he said, pocketing the badge. "And for no other reason."

"The President will see you at four o'clock."

Fowler took a long breath. "Yes, sir," he said and left the Director sitting at the desk as if he had never moved. He switched off his intercom. The door to a side room opened, and a man in a suit came in. Assistant Attorney General Thurmond Arnold sat in front of the desk. "You handled that well."

"I know my people, Mister Arnold. Fowler is a good man and one of the best the Bureau has. He needed to vent his indignation, and as I thought, once he had, his clarity of thinking returned and his patriotism overrode his anger. He will cooperate, as he said, for his country. He'll be no problem."

"That's a relief."

"That's why I've been behind this desk since the Bureau began while insects like you come and go with every change in the wind. Good day, sir."

Sally was at her desk when Dan came in. Their eyes met, and her face reddened, "Dan, I'm sorry. I…"

He held up a hand. "It's okay, Sally. Today, I'd be forgiven anything." He laid his hand on hers. "I have an appointment at four. Are you busy at six?"

She smiled. "I think I can squeeze you in."

THE END

IN CHARGE

Agent Cameron Thomas slammed the heel of his hand on the steering wheel. "Damn it! What's going on up ahead?"

Bill Henning opened the door of the Pontiac sedan and stood on the running board craning his neck. "An accident, maybe. Must have just happened. Nothing's moving."

"We're late already, and now this." Thomas looked over his shoulder and saw headlights glowing behind him from the middle of the Liberty Tunnels to the bridge over the Monongahela River. Ahead of him, taillights filled both lanes to the other end.

"What a mess," said a third agent, Richard Karp.

"What do we do?" said a fourth one, Ronald Blaine.

"We run." Henning grabbed a riot gun from the floor by his feet. "It can't be more than a mile or so. Leave the keys in the car. The cops'll move it." The agents climbed out of the sedan and began threading their way through the traffic jam. Startled motorists stared as the agents ran between the rows of cars, shields held high, two carrying pump shotguns, one carrying an Enfield carbine and one a Thompson submachine gun.

At the mouth of the tunnel, they found a three car pileup that blocked both lanes. They ran out of the tunnel into the traffic. Henning made an executive decision and yanked open the door of a Model A coupe. "FBI," he shouted. "We need your car."

Henning grabbed the speechless driver by his shirt and threw him out onto the pavement. The agents piled in, and Henning bulled through the traffic, scraping fenders and raising hackles. The City cops arrived as the Ford broke through the jam and roared away, Karp on the running board holding a riot gun.

"Where's our backup?" Larry Kendall muttered under his breath. He lowered his binoculars. "They should have been here fifteen minutes ago." He was watching a townhouse across the street through the passenger window of a Bureau car.

"I don't know," Dan Fowler said. "I just hope Wyler doesn't decide to go out for cigarettes or a milkshake before they get here."

A tip from a jilted girlfriend led the agents to a brick townhouse in a neighborhood in the South Hills section of Pittsburgh where bank robber and killer Simon Wyler and his two partners were hiding. Three days before they had robbed the Iron and Glass Bank on Carson Street and killed a guard who already surrendered his weapon. His mistake was pulling a backup piece from his ankle. While the police were canvassing the tri-state area, Wyler and his gang were hiding three miles from the bank.

Fowler and Kendall had been tracking Wyler and his partners for six weeks across three states and lucked out in Pittsburgh. Maisie Brooks, Wyler's cast off girlfriend, was all too happy to tell them where he was hiding.

A sidewalk lamp in the front yard cast a dim light over the brick facade, and light shone from the front window of the town house onto an eight-by-ten patch of grass. The windows were all closed despite the muggy heat. Gauzy curtains let the agents see movement inside but no detail. Someone was definitely home.

"Pittsburgh has the lousiest weather," Kendall complained, wiping sweat from his eyes. "Below zero in February to the nineties in July, and cloudy every day."

"Ever hear of the 'Rope Law?'"

"What's that?"

"In Pittsburgh, it's illegal to sell a Dutchman a rope on a cloudy day."

"Huh?"

"In Holland, it's sunshine and tulips every day. The Dutchmen come here to work in the mills, and the crappy weather makes them suicidal."

"You're pulling my leg."

"The guys from the Pittsburgh office swear it's true."

"Then they're pulling your leg." Kendall looked at his watch. "Seventeen minutes."

He took a pencil from his coat pocket and reached behind his neck. "I hate these vests. They always make me itch in some place I can't reach."

"You'd itch worse from a bullet. I—" Someone was coming down the sidewalk. When he passed through the circle of a street light, Fowler saw he was a teen-aged boy in restaurant whites and a kepi, carrying a brown paper sack. He stepped out of the car and into the boy's path. "Stop, son." He palmed his badge and said, "Federal Agent. What's in the sack?"

The boy stared at the badge as if it were a snake coiled to strike. "Uh, a half a dozen ham sandwiches, French fries, and six bottles of beer."

"Making a delivery?"

"Yeah, from Sammy's Diner." He pointed to the name stitched in red on his shirt.

"Where are you taking it?"

"Six-thirteen. Just down the block."

"Have you delivered there before?"

"A couple of times."

"Who's in the place?"

"I've seen different people. I ring the bell, one of them comes to the door, takes the food, and pays me." He shrugged. "That's it."

"Give me your shirt."

The kid's shirt was a tight fit around Fowler's shoulders. He wasn't happy about going in without his vest, but delivering the food would give him a chance to get a look inside the hideout.

He handed Kendall his wristwatch. "Hang onto this. It's a little too fancy for a counterman."

"What's he going to do?" the kid said, wide eyed, as Fowler shoved a compact .32 revolver into the waistband of his trousers at the base of his spine and covered it with the shirt.

"I'd tell you to watch and see," Larry said, "but you're safer if you duck down in the back seat. There may be bullets flying."

Fowler put the white kepi on his head and strode down the sidewalk whistling "Someone to Watch Over Me." Gershwin was always good luck. He swung the greasy paper sack as if he didn't have a worry. Meanwhile, rivulets of cold sweat were running between his shoulder blades. He stepped onto the stoop of the townhouse and rang the bell. The door opened inward a crack and an eye peered out.

"Yeah?"

"Order from Sammy's Diner."

The door opened wider and Fowler recognized Turk Markham, one of Wyler's gang, by the scar on his jaw. He was wearing the pleated trousers of a cheap blue suit and suspenders over a skivvy shirt in the heat. Turk's right hand was behind the door, and the agent figured there was a gun in it. Turk eyed Fowler. "Where's the kid?"

"Got hit by a car. They took him to Mercy Hospital. Hell of a thing." Dan held out the sack. "Anyway, here's your food. That'll be three dollars and fifty cents." He was hoping Turk would take the bag then reach for his wallet, forcing him to put his pistol aside. No dice.

"Set it on the stoop." Fowler did, the bottles clinking. Turk's free hand went into his trouser pocket and came out with a roll of bills. He thumbed through them one-handed til he found a five.

"Keep the change." He stooped to pick up the sack, and when he did, Fowler got a look over his back. The door opened onto the living room, where a man sat on the sofa reading a newspaper. Simon Wyler sat in shirtsleeves, unshaven, a cigarette dangling from the corner of his mouth. His hair, dyed blonde, contrasted the dark stubble on his face.

Empty beer bottles and a full ashtray shared the coffee table with Wyler's holstered revolver and a half empty fifth of Old Grand Dad.

Turk looked up as a car rounded the corner and passed under a streetlamp. He saw a man on the running board holding a riot gun.

"Oh, shit." He dropped the bag and grabbed Fowler by the shirt and pulled him inside. Fowler stumbled and fell to the floor. He was right about Turk's gun hand. "Simon, it's the Law!" He put his pistol in Fowler's face and said, "Don't move."

"Where's the kid?"

Wyler swore and grabbed for his holster. "Douse the lights." He pointed to Fowler. "What's he doing here?"

"I grabbed him for a hostage. They won't shoot if we have him for a shield."

Outside, the agents watched from the shadows. "Bad timing," Kendall said, aiming his automatic over the hood of the car.

"Bad luck," Henning replied, bringing his shotgun to bear on the front window. The lights went out. Blaine covered the front door with the carbine, while Karp and Thomas ran around the row of townhouses to cover the back.

"Fowler's in there."

"What?"

"He faked a delivery to get a look inside and when they saw you coming down the street, they grabbed him as a hostage."

Inside, Wyler took the shade off a lamp by the window and opened the curtains. He grabbed Fowler by the hair and held him in the opening, gun to his head. "Turn on the lamp then turn it off again."

In the brief flash of light, Kendall and Henning saw Fowler's plight.

"Do you think they know who he is?" Henning said.

"Not likely. If they did, he'd be dead."

Inside the townhouse, a third voice came from upstairs. "What's going on?"

"Cops, Ray," Turk said. "We got a standoff here."

"How do we get out of this?"

"With our soda jerk friend here." Wyler put his hand over Fowler's face and shoved him into an armchair. "Sit down, and don't move."

"Oh, please, Mister," Fowler said, playing scared. "Don't hurt me. I'll do whatever you say,"

"Damned right you will." Wyler peered out the window. "Watch him, Turk." Wyler broke a pane in the window and shouted through it. "All right, boys, who we got out there?"

"FBI," Henning shouted. "You're surrounded, Wyler. Come out with your hands up."

"Don't make me laugh. You saw our hostage. Here's how it's gonna go. Pull your car into the yard and leave it with the engine running. Then stand under the street light where we can see you. We drive away, and you don't follow, or the delivery man dies."

"What do you think?" Kendall said. "If we just pump bullets into the place, we're almost sure to hit Dan."

"If we get them outside we'll have a clear shot at them."

"Yeah, and you fire that shotgun, Fowler'll get sprayed too."

"Blaine was a sniper in the War."

"But could he take down all three before they kill Dan? I say give them the car."

"What else can we do?"

"Not much."

Inside, Ray brought down a valise and set it on the coffee table. "There's the dough." Wyler nodded toward Dan. "Tie his hands, Turk." Turk used a drapery cord to do the job. Fowler was lucky. Turk tied them behind his back, and with his knuckles, Dan could feel the butt of the revolver under his shirt.

Henning pulled Kendall's sedan into the yard and climbed out.

"Now," Wyler shouted, "put your gun on the hood, and step away." Henning hesitated. "Now!" Wyler turned to Turk. "March him outside and keep a gun on him."

Turk held Fowler by the collar and held the muzzle of his automatic under Dan's chin. Turk wasn't taking the scene as casually as Wyler. His eyes darted from shadow to shadow as he stepped outside, holding Fowler in front of him.

Ray followed, carrying the bag with the money in one hand, and an automatic in the other. Wyler was last, carrying a Tommy gun. Unlike Turk, Wyler seemed to take the whole situation as a minor inconvenience. "Steady, boys," he said. "Ray, you drive. Turk, you get in the back with our friend. Move it."

In the dim light, the hoodlums couldn't see Fowler's hands reach under his shirt and his fingers close on the butt of his pistol. He wrapped his fingers around the checkered grips and slid one through the trigger guard. He wasn't nearly as good a shot left-handed as he was right, but his bound hands made it a moot point.

Ray threw the bag into the car and slid under the steering wheel. Turk had to lower his pistol to open the back door, and when he did, Fowler pulled the trigger. He gut shot Turk, who doubled over, and Fowler kicked the gun out of his hand. Wyler swung the Tommy gun around, but before he could pull the trigger, Blaine pulled his. The gangster's head exploded in a spray of blood and shattered bone.

Ray popped the clutch and the car lurched backward, knocking over the sidewalk lamp and broadsiding a parked car. He yanked the gearshift into low. The car windows shattered in a spray of glass as the agents opened fire. The car careened crazily down the street for a hundred feet caroming off parked cars, bounced over the curb, and came to rest against the bole of an elm tree.

Kendall and Henning ran to the car. Henning opened the driver door, and Ray's corpse tumbled over the running board. Kendall breathed a sigh of relief as he saw Fowler, hands still tied, as he stepped into the light of a streetlamp.

"Did you shoot Wyler?" Fowler asked as Blaine untied his hands.

"The guy with the machine gun?" He nodded. "All I could see was heads and shoulders over the car. Lucky you were wearing that white cap."

Neighbors were coming outside. ""What's going on out here?" a man in pajamas and bathrobe demanded.

"FBI," Henning shouted. "Get your ass back inside."

Fowler saw the delivery boy in his undershirt standing across the street. He crossed to him and took off the white kepi. "There's your hat, kid." He looked down at the blood spattered on his shirt. "I'll get the shirt cleaned before I give it back." The boy stared at the hat as if he'd never seen it before. "Oh," Fowler said, reaching in his pocket, "I almost forgot." He handed him Turk's five-dollar bill. "For the food—including your tip."

A thousand miles away, a man named Ronald Armitage was taking his garbage can to the alley. Pickup was Thursday morning in Bedford, Florida, and his wife Myra would give him hell if he missed it. She didn't want the garbage festering for a week in the hot weather, like it did a few weeks before. He had to take a few extra minutes to sweep sawdust and shavings from his workbench in the garage into a paper sack to set out with the can. The rocking horse he was making for his three-year-old granddaughter was almost finished.

The kitchen light was off. It was on when he went outside. Myra must have turned it off. She was sleeping in her armchair in the living room, and he thought he'd have to wake her to get her to bed. He figured that at eighty-two, she was entitled to a nap before bedtime. After all, you don't sleep if you don't need it.

Ronald closed the back door and locked it. He slipped the burglar chain in place as well. Can't be too careful, he thought. In the dim light from the hallway he saw Myra slumped in a kitchen chair. Her eyes were closed, her head leaned against the wall behind her, and her hands lay flat on the table as if she were about to push her chair away from it.

"Now what, honey, are you sleepwalking too?"

Ronald put a hand on her shoulder. Her robe felt damp. He shook her gently. Her head tipped forward and kept on going, landing in her lap. He stared at the bloody stump of her neck and screamed. Ronald stumbled backward, tripping over his own feet. He landed on the flowered linoleum and found himself staring upward into a kewpie doll face framed with long silvery hair. The figure, dressed all in black was holding a very long, very sharp knife.

"What—who?"

"Shh," The figure said putting a finger to paper mâché lips.

Ronald felt the cold edge of the knife at his throat. He felt the bite of the blade. Soon he felt nothing at all.

D.C. was in the throes of a typical summer heat wave. The temperatures hovered in the high eighties most of the day, and the humidity made the air feel like heated gelatin. Fowler carried his suit jacket over his arm as he crossed Constitution Avenue to the Justice Department Building. Only a few years old, the recently finished headquarters was impressive. After a century of moving from building to building, the Department finally had a permanent home in the Federal Triangle. The Bureau moved with it under its new name, Federal Bureau of Investigation and was generally referred to now as the FBI.

Some people criticized the expense of building so impressive a structure with its elaborate mosaics and sculpture in the middle of the Depression, but Fowler realized the need for the people to have a tangible symbol of the power of their leaders and their ability to protect them in difficult times. Over the entrance, the words of Pliny proclaimed, "Everything is created by Law and Order." Maybe not created, Fowler thought, but definitely kept running on the rails.

Inside, he put his jacket back on and straightened his necktie. In a few minutes he'd be reporting to the Director, who stood for no degree of informality.

Fowler's desk was three inches deep with memos, files, and correspondence that came in while he and Kendall were away. He was halfway through the pile when someone knocked on his door. A pretty blonde in a blue linen suit came in, Sally Vane, one of the Bureau's few female agents. The Bureau had an official policy about fraternization between personnel, but Dan and Sally tiptoed around it carefully, and the Bureau turned a blind eye to their relationship.

"You didn't wear a hat today," she said.

"How do you know?"

"Because in sweat weather, it leaves a groove in your hairdo. No groove today; no hat."

"Your powers of deduction are remarkable, Sally."

"Besides, there's no hat on the coat tree. Elementary, my dear Fowler."

"You've been watching Basil Rathbone movies again."

"Where else is a girl going to learn the tricks of the trade?"

"Keep it up, Sally. You'll have your own office in no time."

Her face got serious. "Larry told me what you did to get Simon Wyler. I wish you wouldn't take such chances."

Dan shrugged. "You know the saying: '*Qui audit adipiscitur.*'"

"He who dares, wins," she translated. "How about this one: 'Then love-devouring Death do what he dare.' Shakespeare had it right."

"*Touché.*"

"I love it when you speak French."

"All six words I know. "*Je t'aime, mon cher.*"

"That makes five. What's number six?"

"*Merde.*"

Sally laughed. "Figures."

"May I call you later, *Mademoiselle*?"

"That's seven words."

"Five minutes with you, and I'm improving already."

"Yeah, call me. I'm hungry for crab cakes at Bender's."

As she left, Fowler thought once again how fragile their lives were, and how lucky they were to have each other. He looked at his watch. Time for his meeting with the Director.

The Director sat at his desk, looking as if he hadn't moved since Fowler had been in his office two weeks before. "Sit down, Agent Fowler." The Director always used rank when he addressed his people, a matter of respect and a reminder of who was in charge.

Dan sat in what the agents called the Inquisition Seat directly in front of the massive walnut desk. The Director was a short man, but he compensated by having his high-backed chair placed on a three-inch dais behind the desk. No one looked down on him. It sounded foolish when Fowler first learned of it, but in practice, it had the desired effect. Coupled with his imperious manner, it conveyed the undeniable message that his was the power in that room and beyond.

"You took quite a gamble to put down Simon Wyler and his gang."

"I had faith in the team, sir, and they came through."

"When they finally arrived." Fowler was sure Kendall didn't mention that. The Director seemed to always know every detail.

"They were there when I needed them, sir."

"Yes. All's well that ends well, eh?"

"Yes, sir."

"We have an unusual situation." The Director opened a thick file folder and drew out an eight-by-ten photograph. "What do you make of this?"

The photo showed an older couple sitting at their kitchen table over coffee. At first glance the scene looked normal. Then Fowler realized the woman had a pencil-thin mustache. The man was wearing lipstick and his hair was pulled into a bun. "Are they wearing each other's clothes?"

The Director handed him a magnifying glass. "Look closely."

Fowler felt like a kid peering at one of those comic book puzzles: what's wrong with this picture? Then he saw it. Stitches ringed the throats of both people like Frankenstein's monster. "Good Lord." Their heads had been removed and sewn onto each other's bodies.

"Not only did the killer decapitate these people and switch their heads, he dressed them in clean clothes and posed them like Department store mannequins.

"Where is this?"

"A town called Bedford, Florida."

"When did it happen?"

"The best they can tell, four nights ago,"

"Who are they?"

"The man is Ronald Armitage, a retired accountant. The woman is his wife Myra. He is—was—the uncle of Senator Robert Armitage. The Senator has requested that we look into the case."

Read insisted, Fowler thought. "Not what we normally do."

"I would have politely declined, but ..." The Director took another photograph from the folder.

"Cape Cod, Massachusetts in June."

This one showed an elegant couple sitting on a sofa, one in a tuxedo, the other in a slinky cocktail dress. A luxurious head of blonde hair spilled over the shoulders of the tux. The man's head perched over the gown's décolletage and cleavage between ample breasts.

"Akron, Ohio in May."

He laid a third photo in front of Fowler. This one was shot through the windshield of a car. A pair of teen-agers lay back against the front seat, the head of one on the shoulder of the other. They were naked, at least from the waist up, the boy's butch haircut stood in stark contrast to the bosom below it. The girl's pretty face perched on the broad shoulders of a hard-muscled, athletic body.

"I remember reading about the Albright-Carson murders in Cape Cod, two socialites. There was no mention that the bodies were mutilated."

"Correct. The police have managed to keep the business about the heads out of the press in all three cases. They want that card to play when they have a viable suspect. It's a detail that only he would know."

"This may be a foolish question, sir, but when the victims were buried, were their heads," Fowler fumbled for the right word, "reattached?"

"The victims were autopsied and embalmed, and yes, everything was put back in the right place. You attended the seminar on 'sequence' killers, Agent Fowler. We are dealing with something unique here. You will consult with the local authorities on these cases and assist them." The Director sat back in his chair. "At two o'clock, you will meet with Doctor Taylor Smith, who will also be consulting on the case. Doctor Smith is a psychiatrist who has extensively studied the criminal mind and is working with the Cape Cod Police Department. In the meantime, read through the police reports and familiarize yourself with the situation. Questions?"

Fowler shook his head. "No, sir."

The Director picked up his pipe and began packing the bowl with tobacco. He nodded toward the door.

Dismissed.

Fowler missed lunch because there was so much in the files, and even if he had finished them by noon, he wouldn't have eaten anyway, put off by the disturbing photos and grisly details. It was nearly two when he finished the reports. Their content varied in quality and quantity among the three cities, Akron's information being the most comprehensive, and Cape Cod's the least. He imagined the floundering of resort town cops, used to chasing drunks off the beach, or an occasional purse-snatching or burglary being thrown into deep water without a rope.

His intercom buzzed. "Agent Fowler, Doctor Smith is here to see you."

"Send him in, please." He decided to leave his jacket on the back of his chair and his shirt sleeves rolled past his elbows.

The door opened and Fowler blinked. A woman who could have doubled for Joan Crawford stood on the threshold. She was dressed in a very business-like tan suit, a green cloche hat, and white gloves. Instead of a purse, she wore a brown leather briefcase on a shoulder strap.

"Agent Fowler? I'm Doctor Taylor Smith." She approached with an air of confidence and offered a hand to shake over the desk. Fowler rose from his chair to take it. Her grip was firm but without challenge. It seemed to say, "Maybe you can beat me, but you're smarter not to try it." She met his gaze with a pair of blue eyes the shade of a stove burner with the gas turned low.

"Good to meet you, Doctor Smith."

"Likewise. And please, call me Taylor."

"Then, please call me Dan. As you can see," he said, gesturing to his shirt-sleeves and galluses, "I'm not much for formality, especially in the middle of July."

She laughed. "I concur." She slipped out of her jacket and hung it on her chair. Her build was athletic, not quite mannish; square shoulders, firm arms, and a trim waist.

"You seem very fit," Fowler said.

Smith laughed. "I interned in an asylum in Philadelphia. Some of the patients were, shall we say, 'rowdy'? No, let's say 'violent'. Physical strength was occasionally necessary. I've stayed in shape ever since. There's no better reason than it feels good. You seem very fit yourself."

Fowler smiled at the compliment. She sat in her chair and leaned back, the picture of relaxed comfort, and looked around the room.

"This is a rather Spartan office," she said. "No knickknacks on the shelves, no framed photos on the desk, no pictures on the walls; only government issued furnishings right down to the ashtray."

"What does that suggest?"

"A few things: First, that you are a very private person who keeps himself to himself; you let few people into your life, and few details out, which is likely a necessity in your profession. Second, that you are a self-possessed individual who needs no reinforcement to define yourself, no 'nesting' required for comfort. Third, that you are all business in this room, allowing no distractions. You are a person possessed of equanimity, which is vital in the work that you do."

Fowler felt like an insect under a magnifying glass. He was silent a moment then nodded. "That's fairly accurate. I see why the Bureau called you in for a consult."

She smiled. "I have my moments. Turnabout is fair play. What do you see in me, Dan?"

"I'd rather not form an opinion til I know you better."

Taylor laughed. "Spoken like a true investigator. You deal in the external, the facts of the matter, evidence, the concrete. I deal in the abstract. I suspect that our skill sets will complement each other."

"I hope so. This case is a puzzle."

"The mind is the greatest puzzle, and every one different."

She set her briefcase on her lap and took a legal pad from it. "I took some notes based on the files." Fowler noticed that the top sheet was blank. "I always keep the top sheet empty. You'd be surprised how many people can read upside down, or maybe you wouldn't be."

Fowler nodded acknowledgement. "You've already been on the case?"

"Yes, unofficially; I became interested in it when the Albright-Carson murders hit the newspapers. I offered my help to the Cape Cod force, but by then the Massachusetts State Police had taken over the investigation. Consulting with them, I learned about the case in Akron."

"It's a gruesome business," Fowler said. "Have you ever heard of anything like it before?"

"There have been corpse mutilations probably since Cain and Abel. Sometimes, it's a form of justice. The killer's anger is so great, that taking the life isn't sufficient. Depending on the killer's belief system, the intent apparently was to send the victim into the next life marked for the offense. In Korean culture, a rapist caught by the victim's family instead of the law may be emasculated and his parts sewn to his face. There have been cases in this country in which the Mafia dealt with informants in a similar fashion."

"I could see a revenge motive in this case if it were a single occurrence," Fowler said, "but three couples with no apparent connection over such distances makes that seem unlikely."

"Sometimes revenge isn't a motivation. You've heard of the Massacre at Wounded Knee?"

"The killing of hundreds of Lakota Indians by the Cavalry."

"Yes. It was heinous on its face, but what made it worse was the mutilation of the dead. Soldiers carried off genitalia and women's breasts as trophies, some decorating their hats with them. It was a manifestation of mob mentality, or perhaps mass hysteria like sharks in a feeding frenzy."

"In these cases, I didn't notice a mention of missing body parts in the autopsy reports, just the swapping of heads."

"That's right. There was nothing carried off."

"What would make a killer want to do this?"

"Possibly an emotional trauma from childhood, or authority issues; put-

"It's a gruesome business."

ting the man's head on the woman's body may symbolize a weak father figure or domineering mother. It also may result from abuse by a father; putting the man's head on the woman's body emasculates him."

A knock at the door. Dan could see Sally's hair through the pebbled glass. "Come in." He closed the folder over the photographs as she did.

"I'm sorry," she said. "I didn't realize you were in a meeting."

"Not a problem. Agent Sally Vane, this is Doctor Taylor Smith. She's consulting with the Bureau."

Taylor rose from her chair and shook hands with Sally. The pair eyed each other up and down like two boxers about to go fifteen rounds; no antagonism, just appraisal. "How do you do," Taylor said.

"Pleased to meet you," Sally replied.

"I'm glad to see women accepted into the Bureau as something other than typists or housekeepers. We'll have to compare notes sometime about intruding in the Boy's Club."

"That would be interesting." Then to Fowler, "I need to speak with you on a case issue when you're available. Just ring downstairs for me, would you."

"Sure thing."

Sally left and neither Fowler nor Taylor spoke for a moment. Taylor fished a cigarette case from her bag. "I take it you don't mind if I smoke," she said, pointing at the ashtray with her cigarette.

"Feel free. I may have one myself." He reached in his pocket for his lighter, but she lit the cigarette herself before he could. Taylor took a long drag, held the smoke for a moment, then let it dribble between her lips as she inhaled it through her nose.

"My one bad habit," she said. "I like the taste of the tobacco." She took another drag and said, "How does Agent Vane fit in here?"

"Quite well. She's a thorough professional."

"I'm sure she works twice as hard as most, being under constant scrutiny as one of the few women in the Bureau."

"She does what we all do. She's received the same training and handles the same assignments. She's earned the respect of her fellow agents."

"That's good to hear. It's unfortunate that capable women have to struggle for an opportunity to prove themselves so."

"Has that been true in your case?"

She smiled. "Yes, and it still is, every day of my life. Most of my colleagues see me as a woman first and a professional second. If I weren't attractive, they might not see me at all. Rather than allow it to frustrate me, I view it as one more tool in the box. Tell me, how does Agent Vane respond to the violence of her job?"

"You'd have to ask her. I'd say each of us handles it in his own way, or hers."

"You know, she's very enamored of you."

Fowler blinked. "What makes you say that?"

"Observation; I'm a psychiatrist, and a woman."

"The Bureau has a non-fraternization policy."

"Of course. None of my business, really." She stubbed out her cigarette. "So, how should we proceed with the investigation?"

"On the assumption that all three murders were committed by the same person, what are your theories about the killer might be and how we might catch him—or her?

"I'm pleased that you added 'her,'" Taylor said.

"Until proven otherwise, every possibility is on the table."

"Yet you assume one person is the perpetrator. What if it were two, or three? What if Jack the Ripper had help?"

"I have to start somewhere," Fowler said. "And if I catch one, odds are good it'll lead me to others, if there are others."

"Fair enough."

Doctor Smith offered a variety of perspectives Fowler might not have otherwise considered, most of them non-evidentiary. "Have you considered what phase the Moon was in when these murders occurred?"

"I've read that the Moon affects behavior; that police blotters fill up when the Moon's full, but I hadn't connected it to this case."

"Think about it from a strictly physical standpoint. The human body is about sixty percent water for men, fifty-five for women. That includes blood flow in the brain. If the Moon's gravity can pull something as big as the ocean to make tides, surely it can tug at the blood in the brain and affect the processes there."

"I never thought of that before. I guess it makes sense. How might it bear on these killings?"

"The moon has been in the new phase each murder. It suggests a ritual of some sort."

"I suppose that's possible. Does a ritual mean group participation?"

"Not necessarily. A ritual can as easily be personal as not. You've picked my brain, now let me pick yours. You've read the files and studied the crime scene photos. What do you think?"

"The first thing I normally consider are common elements. Some are obvious, others less so. For example, the same stitch was used to sew all six heads onto the bodies, which points to the same person doing all of them."

"Yes, it's called a loop and lock stitch. It's a common mortuary technique."

"According to the autopsy reports, each couple died in a different way. The teen-agers were asphyxiated by exhaust fumes, parked on some Lover's Lane. Albright and Carson were drugged first, then their throats were cut. The Armitages' throats were simply slit.

"I'd say the teenagers were a crime of opportunity. Maybe the killer found them already dead. If not, maybe he rigged some way to feed exhaust into the passenger compartment. There were so many tire tracks on that dirt road, it's hard to know if they were killed somewhere else and moved or killed there, taken somewhere afterward and brought back."

"What makes you say that?" Fowler said.

"There was almost no blood in the car or at the scene. Albright and Carson were killed in Carson's apartment. Investigators found blood in the bathtub drain, so it looks as if the killer took them one at a time into the bathroom and did his work, washed the mess down the drain and moved on from there."

"And the Armitages?"

"We know from the blood types—his was A positive, hers was O—The wife was killed in the living room. An easy chair was soaked in blood. The husband was killed in the kitchen then the floor thoroughly mopped. Blood was found under the linoleum."

Taylor jotted the information on her pad. "So, different approaches but the *denouement* is the same."

"*Denouement?*"

"French for the climax of a chain of events. It's usually applied to the theater, but I think it's *apropos* in this case, since the bodies are staged in death, a sort of tableau."

"*Apropos*—French for suitable, right?"

"It shares its root with 'appropriate,' yes."

"I'm learning a lot today. Something else to note, none of the heads were hacked off, they were precisely, almost artfully removed. A surgeon maybe?"

"Yes, the killer would have to be careful to be able to sew the heads onto their new bodies; possibly a mortician."

"Right. That would go with the fancy stitching. Another thing, to make so clean a cut, the killer couldn't possibly do it with a jackknife. He'd need something specialized."

"Possibly a Liston knife. We're back to Jack the Ripper again."

"But could it cut through bone?"

"No, a surgeon would use a bone saw." Taylor smiled. "The origin of the nickname 'sawbones' for field surgeons during the Civil War. The autopsy reports didn't mention saw marks on any of the victims, did they?"

"Not that I recall."

"A Liston knife could cut through the muscle, tendons and connective tissue, and a cervical joint could be separated in a number of ways, including manually if the killer has sufficient strength."

"Another thing; these weren't impulse murders. The killer had to do a lot of preparation; the right tools, the right people, the right timing. These murders happened at night, probably to make sure nobody walked in the middle."

"How long would it take to do one of these?"

"I don't know. We'd almost have to try it ourselves."

"Huh?"

"With a corpse from the morgue, a John Doe, maybe, and multiply it by two."

"Let's make that a last resort." Fowler leaned back in his chair and rubbed his eyes with the heels of his hands. "The big question is, will our subject kill again?"

"Based on what I've seen so far, I'd say the answer is an overwhelming yes."

"If your New Moon theory is right, we have less than a month til the next time."

"So, the killer strikes based on the phase of the Moon?" Sally said, forking a bite of crab cake into her mouth. Bender's was crowded, and neither of them was concerned about being overheard in the middle of the clank of silverware on china, thirty conversations, and the cocktail pianist playing clever arrangements of big band tunes.

"That's been the pattern three in a row." Fowler often ran his cases past Sally. He found her insight and differing perspective invaluable, and he knew he could trust her to keep his confidence. "The next step for me is to go to the latest crime scene in Florida."

"When are you leaving?"

"Tomorrow morning."

"Is Larry going too?"

"Yeah, he's already complaining about the heat. Florida's like a steam bath in the summer."

"Too bad the killer didn't wait til February. I'd've gone with you."

"Fortunes of war."

"*C'est la guerre.*"

"Keep it up. You'll have me talking like a Frenchie in no time."

"All part of your never-ending process of refinement." Sally took a sip of her Manhattan. "So how was the lady psychiatrist?"

"Very insightful. She laid out ideas I never would have considered. She's a thorough professional. I felt like she was analyzing me in the bargain."

"It's probably a habit of hers by now. It must have been a real grind, becoming an M.D. first then pursuing psychiatry and fighting male chauvinism every day."

"You wouldn't know anything about that, would you?"

Sally laughed. "Nope, I'm just one of the boys."

"Til you're off the clock."

"Can you think of a better time?"

"Not for my money."

Fowler always marveled at the way Sally could be whipcord tough wearing her badge but all woman when she wasn't. Theoretically, an agent was always on duty, ready to go into action at a call from the Bureau, but rarely was it to run into gunfire and mayhem like city cops or State Police. Sally had proven herself on numerous occasions—even killing a hit man who was about to shoot Fowler—to be as tough and resourceful as any man he'd ever worked with.

"Hey," Sally said. "Is that her?"

"Who?"

"Doctor Smith, the psychiatrist, back by the bar."

Fowler turned his head. "Where? I don't see her, or anybody who even looks like her."

"She moved behind some people. But I'm sure it's her. Either that or Joan Crawford's here for dinner."

Fowler shrugged. "I suppose she shares our taste in good food."

"Or my taste in good men," Sally said, half joking.

Dan laughed. "I wouldn't worry about her. She's married to her career. Besides, you could kick her ass in a fair fight any day."

The pianist started playing "I'm Confessin'" and Fowler held out his hand. "I believe they're playing our song, Miss Vane. May I have this dance?"

"Last week, it was 'Ain't Misbehavin.'"

"That's because every song is our song, Sally." She took his hand, and they joined the handful of couples on the dance floor. For a few moments, the rest of the world went someplace else as they held each other, just a little more tightly than most. The song ended, and as they walked back to their table, in the dim light, Fowler thought he saw Taylor Smith standing in an alcove, but when he looked again, she was gone.

Later, Sally and Dan shared a cigarette as they sat by the Reflecting Pool. The moon was just a sliver at the tip of the Washington Monument, doubled in the water. Couples passed arm in arm, enjoying the pleasant night.

"You're awfully quiet tonight," Sally said, passing the cigarette back to Dan.

"Just thinking about the case."

"I suppose it's hard not to."

"Looking at the moon reminds me that when it's new, the killer may strike again."

"Or he may never."

"In some ways that may be worse. It's ironic. I don't have nearly enough to catch this weirdo and put him away, but the only way I can get more evidence is if he kills again, and that's what I'm trying to prevent."

"I read that Charlie Chaplin once said that irony is 'doing the right thing at the wrong moment.'"

"Sounds about right."

Around the corner of the pool, two young toughs approached a strolling couple from behind. One of them shoved the man and sent him stumbling into the pool. The other grabbed the strap of the woman's purse and tried to pull it from her shoulder. She wouldn't let go.

"Should we?" Sally said.

"Yeah." Dan and Sally sprang from the bench. Both muggers were pulling at the woman's arms as she clutched the handbag to her chest. Her husband climbed out of the shallow water and made the mistake of trying to pull the first mugger away from her instead of punching him in the kidneys or the back of his neck. The mugger twisted his torso and drove his elbow into the boyfriend's forehead. Dan shouted "Hey!" and as the first mugger's head was turning, the heel of Dan's hand was already on its way in a hard thrust to the thug's nose. The mugger let go of the purse and staggered backward, blood spraying between his fingers.

His partner pushed a button and his switchblade knife popped open. Sally caught his right wrist in both hands, twisting them in opposite directions and grinding her thumbnail into the numbing nerves at the base of his hand. The knife clattered on the sidewalk.

The mugger tried to throw a left hook over his trapped forearm. The punch went wide, and using his momentum, Sally pulled him off balance and drove her heel down on his instep. The mugger howled in pain.

The first mugger decided flight was his best option and took off down the sidewalk. Dan's wingtips weren't the best shoes for running, but he caught up with the thug halfway to the Monument. Dan tackled him and they went off the walkway to splash into the pool.

Sally's mugger snarled, "You bitch, I'll kill you." He started for her, his fingers hooked like claws, and Sally's foot came up to connect squarely with his crotch. He doubled over, squealing. Sally grabbed a handful of his greasy hair and pulled his head back. "Shut up." She caught him on the jaw with a roundhouse, his eyes rolled back, and he was out.

Dan and his mugger thrashed in the shallow water. The bottom of the pool was slippery, and Dan's feet couldn't get traction. The mugger broke free and was almost out of the pool when Dan caught his ankles and yanked him backward. The thug's chin hit the sidewalk with a sharp crack, and the fight was over.

By this time, two uniformed Capitol cops were running in Fowler's direction. One of them had his hand on his service revolver, so Dan decided to wait to reach for his shield and instead raised his hands palms forward to show they were empty.

"FBI. I'm Agent Daniel Fowler."

"FBI? Who's he?" one of the cops said, pointing to the unconscious mugger.

"Somebody who thought he could outrun me. Could I borrow your handcuffs?"

In a few moments, both of the purse snatchers were cuffed and on their way to jail.

"I can't thank you enough," the woman, whose name was Edna, said. "We're here from Peoria sightseeing, and I had all of our travel money in my purse. Robert would have carried it in his wallet, but we were afraid of pickpockets."

"Next time, split it up," Fowler said, "different pockets. Don't carry it all in one place."

"I'm embarrassed," said Robert, "that I couldn't protect my wife."

"Don't be," Fowler said. "They ambushed you. Just be watchful."

As they walked away, Sally started laughing.

"What's so funny?"

"You look like a drowned rat."

"Is that any way to talk to a hero?"

As they walked left the Mall, a figure watched from the shadows. Taylor Smith counted to twenty and fell in behind them.

Fowler and Kendall flew as far as Tallahassee where an agent from the local office met them with a car. The heat was bad enough in the capital, but the further south Kendall and Fowler drove, the hotter and stickier it became. Kendall kept the wind wings turned inward, but the humid air blowing in was little relief. The Florida sun turned the Bureau Pontiac into a rolling greenhouse.

"I understand now why they call Florida the Sunshine State, but rain would be good about now," Fowler said.

"And as soon as it stopped, it'd be so humid you'd have to breathe through a snorkel. Tell me again why they sent two of us?"

"My take is the Director wants a 'presence' to satisfy the Senator."

"Ahh, politics."

"Senator Armitage is on the Appropriations Committee."

"It suddenly becomes clear."

They were driving south on Highway 1 and were tired of talking about the "Chop Case" as they'd come to call it, and just about everything else. Fowler shook a cigarette from his pack. "I'm about out of Luckies. We'll have to stop soon."

"Yeah, we could use a fill up, too. I haven't seen any signs for a station in a while, but I've seen plenty for all the tourist attractions."

"Someday, I'd like to drive the length of Florida and stop at all those places; ride the glass-bottomed boat in Silver Springs, visit the Bok Tower bird sanctuary, see the Coral Castle."

"Don't forget the two-headed alligator and the World's Biggest Ball of Twine," Kendall said. "Me, I'd settle for a cold beer on the beach watching the bathing beauties."

"All we have to do is survive to retirement."

Bedford, Florida was ten miles inland from Florida's Treasure Coast. It had around eight thousand people and the population was pretty much the same summer and winter. That far from the Atlantic seashore, it didn't experience the annual influx of winter tourists escaping the northern cold. Citrus groves lined the highway at the fringes.

Fowler had come to judge a city or a town by the number of banks, churches, and funeral homes it had. Bedford had two, four, and one, respectively.

"I wonder if John Ashley robbed either of these two banks," Fowler said as they drove down Bedford's Main Street.

"If you believe the legends, he probably robbed both on the same afternoon."

Along with his gang, Ashley, known as the "King of the Everglades" and the "Swamp Bandit," robbed over forty Florida banks during a nine-year spree of crime between 1915 and 1924, that included hijacking, bootlegging, and even piracy.

"He was unique, that's for sure. He gave ulcers to everybody; the cops, the Mob, the rum-runners, everybody."

"I read he'd rob a bank, then he and his gang would disappear into the Everglades where nobody could find them. He turned into a hero to the poor white crackers because he was a thumb in the eye of the authorities and the landed gentry."

"Like Bonnie and Clyde."

"Here's something I bet you didn't know: his wife's name was Laura Upthegrove."

"You're kidding," Fowler said.

"Nope. That was her last name."

"She probably married Ashley in desperation just to change it."

Kendall shrugged. "We both know ladies love outlaws. Here's the police station."

Their official liaison was an investigator from the Florida Highway Patrol, but Kendall and Fowler had learned from experience that it was good politics and useful practice to recognize the local law enforcement who knew the people and the town far better than any outsider.

Bedford looked like it was designed by Sherwood Anderson. Main Street offered the standard set of shops and stores, a post office, City Hall, and an Atlantic filling station.

"Not exactly a one-horse town," Kendall said.

"Maybe a two-horse."

"You know what the difference is, don't you?"

"Tell me."

"In a two-horse town, you have to be twice as careful where you step."

The Bedford police headquarters was a compact brick building at the south end of Main Street. The sign over the entrance read simply POLICE. Inside, a ceiling fan chased the flies and flapped the papers on the desk of a uniformed officer. The glaze of sweat on his forehead made him look as if he were varnished. He wore a short-sleeved khaki shirt with sewn-in pleats and half moons of sweat in the armpits, tucked into a pair of dark blue trousers. A Sam Browne belt held a holstered revolver. He sat, palms flat on the desk; no hand of solitaire in front of him, no magazine, no crossword puzzle, as if he'd been waiting in that vigilant pose all day for something to happen.

"Can I help you?"

Kendall and Fowler flashed their buzzers and identified themselves. "We'd like to speak with Chief Hargrove."

"Just a minute," the officer said. He stood, and Fowler got a good look at him. He was as compact as the building, all muscle and sinew, and Fowler realized he'd be a handful in a street fight. He disappeared through a door behind him.

"Looks as if they don't have a holding cell," Larry said, pointing to his chin to a high-backed bench like a church pew along the wall to their left. Handcuff rings were bolted to the oak at two-foot intervals.

"Small town, small budget."

"Yeah, with a big crime on its hands."

The door opened, and the officer stood aside, gesturing for the agents to come in. They followed a short hallway to an office with a nameplate that read, Roy G. Hargrove, Chief of Police.

Chief Hargrove was tall and rangy, with big hands and forearms like two-by-fours. He didn't stand or offer a handshake when Fowler and Kendall came in. His graying hair was cropped to his scalp like a shorn sheep in the summer heat, though Fowler suspected he wore it the same year round. Blue eyes glared under a forehead ridged deep enough by his expression to plant a few rows of cotton.

Hargrove's desk was covered with reports, notes, and photographs. On a shelf behind him, Fowler saw books on police procedure, investigation, and law enforcement. "I know why you're here," he said. "The Senator's had every cop in the state barking up my ass, telling me what to do and how to do it. Now he's got you Feds in it too."

"We're not here to tell you how to do your job, Chief Hargrove. We're here to ask what you've done so far and how we may be able like to assist."

"You can assist by catching the crazy bastard who killed Ron and Myra Armitage and get everybody off my back. Since the Patrol took over, I have all the accountability and none of the authority."

"No guarantees, but we'll see what we can do," Kendall said. "I'm guessing the murder rate here is less than the national average."

"The Armitages are the first in twelve years and only the second since I took over as Chief."

"What happened twelve years ago?" Fowler said.

"A wife got tired of her husband beating her up when he got drunk. She waited til he was sleeping off a drunk and beat his head in with a tire iron. This was a quiet, friendly town, and now everybody's locking himself in after supper and sitting with a shotgun pointed at the door."

"I can understand your frustration, Chief." Fowler gestured to the chairs. "Mind if we sit?"

"Sit if you like. This won't take long."

"We've read the Highway Patrol report; we'd like to hear your take on the case. I noticed you have Hanes' *Criminology Handbook* on your shelf. That's required reading for our agents." He went on, "Sutherland's *Principles of Criminology, Criminal Investigation* by Collyer Adam, Morn's *Foundations of Criminal Investigation*; you have the best books."

"And I've read every one of them."

"I commend you for that," Kendall said, "Too many locals don't read beyond the *Police Gazette*."

"We aren't all rubes and hayseeds," Hargrove said. "I was in the Military Police during the War. I take this job seriously."

Fowler wondered why the Chief chose so small a town but began to understand the behavior of the desk officer; Hargrove ran a tight operation and strictly by the book. "Your men were first on the scene, is that correct?"

Hargrove nodded. "One of them, Bill Martin. The neighbors noticed little things, mail sticking out of the box, a couple newspapers on the front porch, the empty trash can still at the curb, and Ron's car sitting in the driveway. Bill knocked at the front door, and nobody answered. He went around back and saw them sitting at the table like you see them in the crime scene photos. That and the flies. There were flies all over the place."

"There was no sign of forced entry," Kendall said. "Was the door locked?"

Hargrove nodded. "Bill went in through an unlocked window. The front door was locked from the inside and the security chain in place. Likewise the kitchen door."

"So we can't rule out the victims knowing the killer."

"I read in the Patrol's report that fingerprints at the scene were inconclusive," Kendall said. "Plenty of prints in the house besides the victims'."

"That's right. They had lots of visitors. They were popular. Everybody knew them. Ron was the Postmaster for twenty-two years before he retired, and Edna was active in every community organization but the Men's Club. This has been a shock to the whole town."

"Does anyone but you and your officers know about the decapitations?"

"No one except Ralph Greene, the Coroner. He's also the local undertaker. I told my men not to say a word about it even before the state boys did."

"It looks to me that you did a thoroughly professional job, Chief," Fowler said. Kendall nodded in agreement. "Could we take a look at the house?"

"I'll take you there myself." Hargrove opened a desk drawer and took out a key. "Let's go."

They rode in Hargrove's car, an older Ford sedan painted black and white with the words Bedford Police in a circle around a star on the front doors. The sky was beginning to cloud up, darker to the east. "Rain's coming," Hargrove said.

"We're in hurricane season aren't we?" Kendall asked.

Hargrove nodded. "Til November. But it's usually not as bad as people think. It's not an everyday thing."

"I guess the worst was Labor Day of thirty-five, huh?"

"It was the worst the state ever saw. We didn't have the destruction in

Bedford that some places did, but we got our share of damage. Nobody died in Bedford, but everybody here had a friend or a relative who died somewhere else." He looked to the east. "Just a summer thunderstorm. It'll rain like fury a while and the sun'll be out before you know it."

The Armitage house was only a few blocks from the police station on a street lined with one-story homes, most of them stucco painted white or in light shades of tan or green. A variety of shrubs and bushes lined the sidewalks along with a few pine trees and palms. "Not much shade here, is there?" Fowler said.

"Not much cover, either," Kendall added.

The house was set back a little farther from the street than most, beyond a front yard of browning St. Augustine grass. Flower beds flanked the stoop and the front door, and the place looked like just another Florida house until you saw the crime scene notice tacked to the front door.

Inside, the air was close because the windows were all shut and latched. A faint coppery scent of blood hung in the air.

"Back here." Hargrove led them past the ruined easy chair in the living room down a short hallway to the kitchen that Fowler recognized from the photographs. Except for the missing bodies, the scene looked the same, as if the couple had finished their coffee and gone grocery shopping or to visit neighbors.

"Everything was dusted for prints?"

Hargrove nodded. "Everything."

"Have you ruled out robbery as a motive?"

Hargrove nodded again. "Don had thirty-two dollars in his wallet, and Myra's jewelry still in a fancy box on her dresser."

Fowler leaned over the table. A saucer held a blob of wax, a burned down candle, melted wax spread over the porcelain and the charred stub of a wick. He sniffed at it. "Cinnamon. Why burn a candle?"

"Part of the staging," Kendall suggested. "But if I wanted to make the scene look romantic, I'd put out wine, not coffee."

"Or to cover up the smell when the bodies started to get ripe," Hargrove said. "So people wouldn't notice so soon."

"Good point, Chief," Fowler said. He looked closer at the wax in the saucer. "Look at this: there's something under the wax."

"It's a paper match, probably used to light the candle."

Fowler opened his pocketknife. He was about to cut the wax away from the match when Hargrove said, "Should you do that?"

"I won't tell if you don't."

"You can't get prints off a match, The paper's too coarse."

"You're right, but this isn't an ordinary match." Fowler held it up for the others to see. The match was wider than most, almost double width and from its base to the charring ran the tiny letters UNCL."

"This is from a specialty matchbook. Night clubs and restaurants have them made with wide matches inside, usually printed with the name of the club on each one, at least in the front row. The question is: was it here when the killer

"Not much cover either."

arrived, or did he bring it with him?"

"And where is it now?" Kendall said. "When the investigators bagged up evidence, did they find a matchbook?"

"Not that I know of," Hargrove said. "I didn't see it on the evidence list. They probably wouldn't pay it any mind."

"If it was already here, I don't imagine the killer would have lit the candle then put the matchbook back where he found it. Too much going on. I'd say he brought it with him." Fowler studied the match again. "'UNCL,'" Uncle. Are there any local nightclubs or restaurants with Uncle in the name?"

"Not around in Bedford, but maybe close. I can find out."

"That would be helpful."

The rain started as they drove back to the station, big fat drops that the pelted the windshield so hard the wiper could hardly keep up. Forks of lightning flashed across the dark sky and thunder boomed like cannon fire.

"Two seconds," Kendall said. "What's that clock out? A half mile away?"

"Give or take," Hargrove said. "Rule of thumb is five seconds a mile." He was silent a moment. "It makes me sick," the Chief continued. "Why my town? All these years I've kept this town safe, known these people all my life, and now I have to look at each one as a suspect."

Kendall and Fowler shared a look and an unspoken decision. "Don't blame yourself. We don't think the killer's a local person. The Armitages are third in line. That's why we're here."

Hargrove's head whipped around. "There were others like this?"

"In different parts of the country. They didn't tell you because they were told not to."

"The sons of bitches."

"We're telling you because you deserve to know, but you can't tell anyone else. Not yet."

Hargrove nodded slowly and gave a thin smile. "That's good to know, in one way, anyhow. Thank you."

Lightning flashed, and the clap of thunder was instantaneous. The storm was there. Fowler wondered where it would arrive next.

The answer was Georgia, where the weather made Florida's rain look like April showers and turned the night flight back to D.C. into a carnival ride.

The plane lurched and bounced Fowler off his armrests.

"I'll flip you for who gets to shoot the pilot," Kendall said.

"Be my guest. But wait til we land first."

When Fowler arrived in his office a day later, he found the usual stack of paper on his desk; memos, reports and files. He was halfway through the memos when Sally tapped at the door. Fowler smiled, happy for the distraction.

"Every time I go away, I come back and find a fresh pile of papers on my desk. Now there's a mystery,"

"No mystery," she said with a laugh. "It's the 'refrigerator principle of bureaucracy.'"

"Huh?"

"Why were refrigerators invented?"

"I'm sure you're going to tell me something I didn't know."

"To delay the need to make substantial decisions. Do I keep the leftovers from tonight's pot roast, or do I throw them away? Put them in the refrigerator, and you don't have to decide."

"For a while. So how does it apply to bureaucracy?"

"When somebody has an issue he doesn't want to be bothered with and its liable to stink, he writes a memo, sends a letter with questions he 'needs' answered before he can deal with the problem or in some other way throws the ball to somebody else. That way, he doesn't have to think about it for a while. He puts it in the refrigerator so it doesn't start to smell bad while he drags his feet. If he's good enough at it, by the time he retires, it'll still be there, and someone else will have to clean out the refrigerator."

"That's brilliant. Won't work for me though. I can imagine me facing off against a bank robber and saying, 'Hold on a minute, I need you to answer a few questions before I decide whether to shoot you in the leg or the head.'"

Sally laughed. "That's because you're not a desk jockey, Dan. You do the real work around here."

Kendall came in. "I think every third man in Florida is somebody's uncle and runs a business." He read from a list. "Uncle Billy's Roadside Emporium, Uncle Ray's Chicken Shack, Uncle Bart's Alligator Farm, Uncle Bob's Swamp Tours, Uncle Buck's Auto Repair. Shall I go on?"

Fowler said, "I get the picture. Where'd that list come from?"

The Tallahassee office. It's from the DBA—Florida's 'Doing Business As' list of registered names."

"How many hand out matchbooks?"

"They're working on it."

"Am I allowed to ask why you're looking for matchbooks?"

"No, but I can tell you. I know you won't blab." He turned to Larry. "Kick the door shut, will you."

Fowler gave Sally a thumbnail sketch of the case to date. "The matchbook wasn't at the scene, so we figure the killer took it with him, maybe brought it too. It's a lead, but a pretty thin one."

"We're there candles at the other murder scenes?"

"There were no candles at the Akron scene; it was a car on a rural road. Hold on." Fowler took a file from his desk drawer and thumbed through a set of photographs. He studied one for a moment and set it on the desk. "This is the Cape Cod crime scene."

The photo showed an expensively furnished living room with a well-dressed couple sitting on the high-backed sofa. On the coffee table was a bottle of brandy and two snifters. The man sat in a leisurely pose, legs crossed, ankle to knee and an arm around the woman.

"I'm glad you told me about the heads before you showed me this."

"Look at the wall behind them, on top of the credenza. There are two candle sticks. Neither candle has been lit."

"So burning candles aren't some kind of fetish for the killer." Sally looked closer. "There are cigarettes in the ash tray. I count three. Are they all the same brand?"

Fowler leafed through the Cape Cod report. "No mention of brand, but one was laced with marihuana."

"It's still legal," Kendall said, "but not for long. There's a push to ban it in the U.S. Maybe these two were using up their supply while they could."

"Habits of the idle rich," Fowler said. "The man is Kenneth Albright, one of those fortunate folks who inherit for a living."

"Albright Shipping?"

"That's the family. The woman is Roberta Carson, her family are Old New York bluebloods. According to the scandal rags, they were an item."

"It's bizarre," Kendall said. "There's no obvious connection among the victims. In fact it's almost as if the killer planned it that way."

"Maybe he did."

The phone rang. Fowler picked it up. "Yeah?"

The operator's voice crackled on the line. "Call for you Agent Fowler. A Doctor Smith."

"I'll take it in a minute. I'll talk to you later, Larry. Sally, thanks for your insight. I'll check on the cigarettes."

They left, and Fowler toggled the phone. "Fowler."

"Hello, Dan. How are you?"

"Doctor Smith, I'm doing well. What can I do for you?"

"I'm interested in what progress you're making on the case. I realize you can't discuss it over the telephone, so I thought we could arrange to meet. I have a few ideas I'd like to air with you."

"I just got back in the office this morning. I can't today. Just a minute." He thumbed through his leather bound agenda. "Tomorrow, I have a meeting in the morning, but the afternoon is clear. One o'clock in my office?"

"That will be fine."

"I'd like to include my partner, Agent Kendall."

Smith hesitated a moment then said, "Of course. If anything changes, please call me. I'm staying in the Sofitel in Lafayette Square. Room nine-twelve."

"I'll do that. By the way, did I see you at Bender's two nights ago?"

"Yes. I love good seafood. The desk clerk recommended the place. The crab-stuffed flounder was terrific. Sorry I didn't see you. You should have come over and said hello. I hate eating alone, but as much as I have to travel, it happens a lot."

Fowler brushed the comment aside. "Yeah, I like their crab cakes myself. Well, I'm up to my ears in work right now, so I'll plan on seeing you tomorrow."

Fowler hung up the phone. *Something odd about that one*, he thought. He supposed that when you spend your days rooting around in the motives of madmen and murderers, it shapes your personality in odd ways. Then he realized that the same could probably be said of himself. "Dan, old boy," he said out loud, "you need a vacation."

Dan and Larry agreed they'd gain little by traveling to Akron or Cape Cod. The crime scenes were cold, and the police in both places had done as much as could be, although, as Larry said, "I must say that Cape Cod in July sounds inviting, especially on the Bureau's dime."

"With our luck, the next murder will probably happen in Death Valley."

"Sounds appropriate."

That afternoon, they found out it was a lot closer.

Mildred Cavanaugh fished in her purse for the key to the Bennet Real Estate Agency office in Wytheville, Virginia. The office was closed on Wednesdays in the summer. Jim Bennet liked to play golf, and figured if he had to be in the office on Saturdays to accommodate customers, he was entitled to a day on the golf course. He called it his "mid-week weekend" and was generous enough to allow his secretary, Janice Watts the day off, since she worked a full day Saturday, too. That gave Mildred a morning to do her routine cleaning of the office.

She pushed the door open with her substantial rump and carried her bucket and vacuum cleaner into the waiting room. There were no special instructions on Janice's desk, so Mildred would just do the regular routine of dusting, sweeping, emptying the wastebasket, and generally tidying the office, "redding up," as her Irish mother always put it.

She set down her things and opened the door to the inner office. For a second, in the dim light, she thought she was intruding on a meeting. Then she realized it was Janice behind the desk, but it wasn't really Janice. The pretty brunette's head was resting on Jim Bennet's thick torso. Bennet's head sat on Janice's slender body in a chair, a steno pad in her lap and a pen held loosely in her fingers.

The carpet was sticky with blood, and when Mildred stepped backward, she slipped and fell, covering herself in it, so that when she ran screaming into the street, people thought she'd been stabbed or worse.

Fowler's phone rang around nine-thirty. "Dan, it's Larry. We got another one." Kendall's voice was so urgent that Fowler didn't have to ask another what. Instead, he said instead. "Where?"

"Wytheville, Virginia."

"We can be there in five or six hours. Call down for a car."

In fifteen minutes Fowler and Kendall were on the road to Wytheville.

"There'll be no keeping a lid on this one," Kendall said, "Thanks to the cleaning lady the whole town from the mayor down to the fire chief's Dalmatian knows about the decapitations."

"That's not good. The press'll play it up big and cause a panic. But I guess we couldn't keep it a secret forever. I was hoping we could use that detail to nail down the suspect, something only he would know."

"That's wishful thinking, Dan, that we'll have a suspect. This guy's all over the map."

"So the killer's a traveler; maybe a rail worker, a truck driver, or just a hobo."

"Pretty sophisticated technique for a vagrant," Kendall observed.

"Maybe not. The Depression kicked people out work from every rung on the ladder, maybe the killer was a doctor once, or an undertaker."

"What if he's a traveling salesman? I can hear the jokes now: did you hear the one about the traveling salesman who killed people and switched their heads?"

"That's not funny, Larry, but I'll bite. What's the punch line?"

"He was good at changing people's minds."

Fowler rolled his eyes.

"How about 'he put a whole new face on things'?"

"If you're going to keep that up, pull over and let me out. I'll walk to Wytheville."

"Dan, if you can't keep your sense of humor on this job, you'll go nuts in a week. You'll end up on that headshrinker's couch, although that might not be a bad place to be if she's sitting beside you. I saw her coming out of your office."

"Taylor Smith? She's a looker, but I can't relax around her. I feel like she's analyzing every twitch of my eyebrow."

"I guess that's the habit you fall into in her profession. It's true of us too. I see a guy on the street, in a bar, on a train, and I catch myself taking his measure, wondering if he's good in a fight, where he got that scar over his eyebrow, where he could be hiding a gun or a knife."

"But with us, it's a survival skill. With her, it's like a game or a puzzle."

"We're all in the 'solving' business, I guess, when you think about it."

"This murder knocks down Smith's Moon idea, but you may be onto something about an out of work doctor or carcass mechanic. What would knock a doctor off his pedestal?"

"Maybe he's a drunk, or a hop-head," Kendall said. "Dope would explain loss of his shingle and crazy behavior."

"Maybe, but I can't imagine someone making those precise cuts and stitches in a narcotic stupor."

"You saw *Reefer Madness*. Maybe it pumps him up, makes him want to kill."

"This whole case gives me a headache." Fowler turned on the radio, leaned back in his seat, and put his hat over his eyes. "Wake me up when we get to Wytheville."

But Fowler didn't sleep right away. He kept thinking, what if this and what if that, following every possible line of thought and hitting one dead end after another. The case was drawing him in and taking over his mind.

"Wytheville, this stop is Wytheville," Kendall quipped in a conductor's drone. Fowler blinked awake. He looked out the window to see a bustling mid-sized city right out of *The Saturday Evening Post*. Federal Route 11 doubled as the city's Main Street. Where Bedford looked like a creation of Sherwood Anderson, Wytheville was more Sinclair Lewis. Everybody on the street looked as if he were going to a Rotary Club meeting. They passed a Civil War Monument with a Confederate flag flying over it and drove through a five block business district, lined with cars parked nose into the curb and multi-story buildings, including the George Wythe Hotel. "We can get rooms there if we have to stay over," Kendall said.

They had called ahead and were expected by the Virginia State Police Field Office Number 4, whose building stood at the western end of Main street. The corporal at the desk led them down a long corridor to an office and tapped on the door.

"Come in."

The office was smaller than Fowler's but not by much. The windows were open and bees buzzed in the magnolias beyond the screens. Behind the desk sat a uniformed officer. The heavy brass nameplate on the desk read: CAPTAIN NOAH SANGSTON. On his side of the desk a man in a rumpled grey suit leaned back in a chair, a cigarette between his fingers. His thinning hair was brushed back from his forehead to cover a growing bald spot at his crown.

"Gentlemen," Sangston said. "Welcome to Wytheville. I'm Captain Sangston, and this is Detective Trumbull. We have one hell of a situation here, and I'm hoping that between us we can work it out."

Sangston had one of those command voices that delivered his words in a cadenced rhythm at a near monotone, but could suddenly crack like a whip with equal effect. Fowler figured, based on that and his trim physique that he, like Chief Hargrove, was ex-military.

"I understand this m.o. is not unique."

"No, Captain, this is the fourth such case in three months," Fowler said.

"That we know of," Larry added.

"Normally we wouldn't intervene in a City case, jurisdictions being what they are, but the Wytheville Department realized immediately that this case is over their heads. Frankly, I think they're relieved we took over. Detective Trumbull is in from Headquarters to handle things from our end. I'm a simple person. I don't go in for pissing contests. We all have the same objective, to catch this crazy son of a bitch. We're willing to share and cooperate, but we expect the same."

"Agreed," Fowler said.

Trumbull flicked his ash in the tray. "Tell us what you've got."

For the next fifteen minutes, Fowler and Kendall related the details of the case. "We were just apprised of your victims a few hours ago," Kendall said, "We came immediately."

Trumbull said, "The biggest complication we have is that word got out about the heads. You know what sensational rumors are like, and what they can do to a case. The phone calls are already coming in from all over, and the photographer from the *Wytheville Enterprise* has all but pitched a tent on the sidewalk outside Jim Bennet's office."

"What relationship did Bennet have with his secretary?" Kendall asked.

"Strictly business. He was what we might politely call a 'confirmed bachelor.' Janice Watts was a middle-aged divorcee. We don't know of anything going on between them."

"So no jealous spouses," Fowler said.

"Right. The Coroner figures the murders occurred sometime last evening, after office hours. I have men going over the appointment book right now to determine who might have been there."

"That's something we didn't have before, "Fowler said."But so is the phase of the Moon and the fact that the previous victims are husband and wife, or boyfriend and girlfriend."

Sangston shook his head. "It makes no sense."

"It doesn't have to," Kendall said. "Crazy people do crazy things."

"And we get to clean up the mess."

Trumbull stood. "I suppose we should go over to the crime scene."

"Take a look at it, think about it, and we'll talk again," Sangston said.

Bennet Insurance was only a few blocks away, a buff brick building butted cheek to cheek with a dentist's office to the left and a stationery store to the right. The street was closed to traffic, and both state and local police cars were clustered around the crime scene. Uniformed city officers held rubberneckers at a distance. Fowler noticed some of them with cameras and several with Press passes in their hatbands.

"How many newspapers do you have in Wytheville?" he asked.

"One," Trumbull said. "The rest are out-of-towners. Word gets around fast when something really bad happens."

Kendall shook his head. "The evil that men do."

"There he is!" one of the reporters shouted. When the reporters saw them, the frantic questions flew. "Detective Trumbull! Detective Trumbull!" they shouted.

""They know your name. You must be famous," Kendall said.

"This afternoon. Goes with being in charge."

"Are there any leads yet?" one of the reporters called. Another said, "Who are these men?" A third: "Were they really decapitated?"

Trumbull turned toward the reporters and said, "You'll hear all about it later. Let us do our job."

A handful of men, some uniformed and some in street clothes were methodically combing the waiting room for anything remotely resembling a clue. One of them, a thin man in shirtsleeves and wire rimmed glasses came over. Trumbull introduced him as Detective Hargiss.

"Not much yet," Hargiss said. "But we'll keep looking. Our best bet's the date book."

The inner office was a little larger than the anteroom, and was furnished a notch higher in quality. The guest chairs were upholstered, the desk was walnut, and the floor was carpeted. The room was windowless, but a landscape painting of a waterfall surrounded by forest compensated for it.

The bodies had been removed, but the scene looked no less ghastly. Nearly everything in the place from the desktop down was spattered with or soaked in dried blood. "Looks like they gave up all twelve quarts," Kendall said.

One-by-twelve planks had been laid on the floor to form a walkway. "We did that to keep our footprints to a minimum in the carpet. The blood dried and left some pretty good impressions. Except for the cleaning lady's shoe, all of them are the same, a size eleven brogan."

"Big guy," Fowler said.

"We also found a few prints on the linoleum in the hallway leading to the alley out back. We figure that's where the killer left. There's no blood or tracks in the front."

"What's back there?"

"A small powder room and an alcove with shelves full of office supplies. Come on, I'll show you."

"No bathtub to do the cut work," Kendall looked at the powder room. "That explains the mess in Bennet's office."

Six footprints led from the office to the alley door, fading as they went, like a rubber stamp that hadn't been re-inked. The word Florshiem showed in the heels.

Fowler crouched for a closer look. "Expensive."

"And new," Kendall added. "The heel print is sharp."

"Something's not right with these prints. They're too close together."

"What do you mean?" Kendall said. "They look far enough apart to match a tall man's stride. Rule of thumb, a man's stride is close to his height."

"The prints are far enough apart lengthwise," Fowler said, "but not widthwise. Somebody that tall should have proportionate hip bones, a wider spread between his feet."

"So we're looking for a tall, skinny killer with big feet," Larry muttered.

"Maybe so, but it still looks wrong to me."

"We figure the killer went out the back door and down the alley," Trumbull said.

"What's upstairs?"

"An apartment that Bennet rented out, but it's empty right now. The tenants moved two weeks ago, a young married couple."

"Did they leave on good terms?"

"We're following up on that angle now."

"And nobody on the street saw anything?" Fowler said.

"Not that we've heard so far, but it's been less than twenty-four hours."

"About that, what did the Coroner say was the approximate time of death?"

"He estimated around seven to nine o'clock last night. We asked him to hurry the autopsies. He should be done soon if he isn't already."

"Let's pay him a visit."

When they hit the sidewalk, a reporter with a pass identifying him as belonging to the *Washington Post* said, "Holy cats, guys, that's Dan Fowler, the guy who saved the President! Agent Fowler! Agent Fowler! Why's the FBI on the case?"

Flashbulbs popped as cameramen, eager for anything to photograph after a long hiatus, captured Dan, Larry and Trumbull in a dozen shots. The reporters followed them down the sidewalk to the car, all tossing questions at once so none could be singled out from the babble.

Trumbull turned to the reporters, waving his arms. "Not now, fellows. We'll be releasing a statement later."

"Let us do our job," one of the news hounds, a red-faced guy in a bad toupee said.

"As soon as we do ours," Trumbull replied.

They climbed into the car and drove away, leaving the reporters still shouting questions.

"The curse of fame," Kendall said to Trumbull. "That's what happens when your picture's on the front page one time too many. Makes it harder to sneak up on the bad guys."

Trumbull drove them several blocks to Wytheville General Hospital. He parked behind the building and led them through a door into a lower level and the County Morgue, which was a single large room, white-tiled, brightly lit, and as scrupulously clean as a surgery.

Two bodies lay on examination tables, Y-cuts roughly stitched shut on each chest. The pretty brunette's head looked grotesque over Bennet's hairy chest, but nowhere near the incongruity of Bennet's very masculine head over her breasts.

"Looks like Tiresias," Kendall said.

Fowler snorted and Trumbull blinked. "Who?"

"Long story. Tell you later."

The Coroner, Doctor Goldberg, was a tall, rawboned man, whose tan testified to plenty of time outdoors. Fowler figured golf or tennis. Introductions were made and Goldberg began his spiel. "The cause of death is obvious. What isn't is what led up to decapitation. Neither showed signs of a struggle. We're examining the blood, what of it was left, for narcotics or other substances that would render the victims helpless. I did find something on Bennet's neck. I almost missed it because of the stitching; a tiny puncture wound, maybe a hypodermic needle."

"And the woman?" Kendall asked.

"I haven't found one on her, but if she were subdued in the same way, the needle mark may have been destroyed when her head was cut off, or covered by the stitching."

"About the stitching," Fowler said. "What does it tell you about the killer?"

"The neck muscles were attached by heavy cross-stitching, then the skin sewn shut by a very precise lock stitch. Surgeons who are trying to avoid heavy scarring or morticians who are trying to make a cadaver more presentable for viewing might use the technique. I might add that the job on both was meticulous. Very neat work by what appears to be a practiced hand."

"How long do you think it might have taken?" Trumbull said.

"It's hard to tell. This was no hack job. The killer took his time and paid close attention to detail. It may have taken several hours."

There were sounds of commotion in the hallway. The press gang had followed the agents to the hospital. The double doors swung open and reporters and cameramen burst in struggling with two orderlies and a uniformed security guard.

Goldberg quickly pulled sheets over the bodies. "What is the meaning of this?" he shouted.

"Freedom of the press, Doc," one of them said. "The public has a right to know."

Goldberg grabbed the man by his lapels and lifted him til his feet dangled over the tiles. "Get out of here, you scum." he hissed in the reporter's face.

A flashbulb popped, and one of the cameramen cackled, "Got it! There's a front-pager."

Kendall wrestled the camera away from him. The photographer grabbed for it, but Fowler shoved him back. Kendall pulled the plate from the camera and threw it on the floor then ground it under his heel.

Trumbull flashed his badge. "Everybody out, or I'll arrest you all for trespassing."

Larry pushed the camera into the sputtering photographer's chest. "The name's Kendall, K-E-N-D-A-L-L. Make sure you spell it right." The cameraman muttered a curse under his breath and backed away. The orderlies herded them into the corridor, and in a moment, the press dogs were gone.

"I'm sorry, Doctor Goldberg," the security guard said. "They came in through the Emergency Room and were down here before I could stop them."

"It's not your fault, Ernie. Those vultures have no respect for the living

"I almost missed it because of the stitching; a tiny puncture wound."

or the dead."

"I'll stand down the hall to make sure they don't come back."

"Thank you." Then to the agents. "I understand that there have been other murders like this one. Is that true?"

"Yes, it's true," Fowler said. "This is number four."

Goldberg closed his eyes and shook his head. "Dear God," he said. "Four."

"We're going to have to ask you to hold the bodies for the time being," Trumbull said. "Neither of them has immediate family here, so I don't expect any urgent demand for release. If you think you'll need it, I'll have some City uniforms down here to keep the nosy away."

"I'd hope that wouldn't be necessary, Detective, but it probably is. I'm sure a photograph of the two victims would sell a lot of newspapers. I have to admit that I'm shaken by this. I thought I'd seen every kind of horror; bodies mangled in auto accidents, a utility worker with his face burned off by high voltage, a hunter savaged by a mountain lion. None of them were as distressing as the cold, perverse precision of this bastard. I hope you catch him before he does something like this again."

"We're trying," Fowler said.

"No punishment is enough for something like this." Goldberg took off his glasses and rubbed his eyes. "This will haunt me for the rest of my life. When you find him, don't arrest him, just shoot him, and while you're at it, put an extra bullet in him for me."

Fowler, Kendall, and Trumbull left the hospital by a side door to dodge the reporters. "Let's go back to the Field Office. I have people going through Bennet's agenda to determine who he saw yesterday. Questioning them might turn up something."

"When all else fails," Kendall said, "follow procedure."

When they arrived at the Field Office, the corporal at the desk said, "Detective Trumbull, the Captain said he wanted to see you as soon as you arrived, and a message came for you, Agent Fowler." The corporal handed him a folded slip of paper. Fowler read it and frowned.

"Good news or bad?" Kendall said.

"Depends," Fowler answered. "It's from Chief Hargrove in Bedford. The match we found at the Armitage house came from Uncle Billy's, a seafood shack in Port St. Lucie, twenty miles away. His people searched the house from top to bottom and didn't find the matchbook."

"What's that all about?" Trumbull asked.

"At the murder scene in Florida, we found an unusual match but not the matchbook. The killer may have carried it in with him, or maybe found it in the house and took it as a souvenir. Now we know where it came from."

"It could mean the killer was local," Kendall said, "but that's questionable because the other murders occurred so far apart."

"Following the traveler theory," Fowler said, "it's possible the killer passed through Port St. Lucie or even stayed there."

"That's frustrating," Trumbull nodded. "Every lead splits off into more possibilities."

"Like the Hydra in Greek myth," Fowler concurred. "Chop off one head and two grow back in its place. Anyway, Hargrove said he knows the Chief in Port St. Lucie and he'll personally follow up on it."

"That's good. We need all the help we can get."

"Captain Sangston's waiting," Trumbull said.

Sangston sat in shirtsleeves, his necktie pulled down, poring over a stapled sheaf of papers. A cold cigar sat in the ashtray beside an empty coffee cup and a half-eaten sandwich.

"I got a call from the editor of the *Roanoke Sentinel*," he said, "complaining about a physical confrontation between investigators and reporters."

"That was quick," Kendall said. "You'll probably get more."

"The best of them are jackals. I heard their side. Now tell me what really happened."

Trumbull recounted the intrusion into the morgue and the agents' reaction and finished with, "I would have done it myself, but Kendall beat me to it."

"Three things, Captain," Kendall said. "One, we can't have the press fanning this; the case is tough enough already. They had to be put in their place. Two, the survivors deserve some decency. Three, in a week Dan and I will be gone and forgotten. Local officers will have to deal with them til retirement. Better we be the heavies."

"I agree." Sangston pushed back his chair. "Tell me what you found."

"Not much your people hadn't found already," Fowler said. "The differences between this case and the others are puzzling. These victims had no romantic relationship that we know of. The previous murders happened on the New Moon; this one's early. Bennet and his secretary were staged, like the others, but not cleaned up."

"We have a name from Janice Watts' datebook. I didn't want to prejudice your eyes with it before you saw the crime scene. A Drew Morgan had an appointment with Bennet at six-thirty last night."

"That's unusual," Kendall commented, "after the office is closed."

"Not really," Trumbull flicked his cigarette at the ashtray. "Bull's-eye! Selling houses isn't like Macy's. You make yourself available when the clients are. The datebook shows a dozen appointments at odd hours. This Drew Morgan may be the killer. We're running down the name now. So far, we've got zip."

"No Mister, Missus or Miss?" Fowler asked.

Trumbull shook his head. "Could be male or female. That complicates things even more."

"Or it may not," Fowler said. "We keep referring to the killer as 'he.' What if we're mistaken? What if the killer's a woman?"

"A woman?" Sangston echoed. "Why would you think so?"

"Something I saw in Bennet's office: the killer tracked blood on the floor leading to the alley door. The prints were of a size eleven shoe and far enough apart to indicate a tall man's stride. But the prints were close together width-wise, indicating a smaller person. Maybe the killer wore oversized shoes and left those prints to throw us off."

"If that's the case, it could as easily have been a small man," Sangston suggested.

"And a clever one who knows something about investigation."

"But would a woman be strong enough to manhandle the corpses, especially after rigor mortis set in?"

"Rigor mortis usually lasts no longer than four hours at the outside," Kendall said. "Our killer was in no hurry. The office was closed, and neither Bennet nor Watts would be missed immediately. He—or she—had plenty of time to get things done. And as for strength, I've known a few farm girls who could throw me like a bale of hay."

"So now," Sangston added, "we've just effectively doubled the number of potential suspects."

Someone knocked at the door. The corporal came in with an envelope. "Detective Trumbull, Trooper Clay said to give this to you immediately. He found it in the alley outside Jim Bennet's office."

Trumbull opened the envelope and pulled out what looked like a slim black cord. At either end was a half-inch piece of metal pointed at one end and squared off at the other. The cord passed through a tiny triangle of something white, trapped by the metal. He turned it over in his hands then handed it to Fowler. "Any ideas?"

Dan felt the cord between his fingers then tugged at it from both ends. It stretched. "Elastic. Unless I'm mistaken, this is a cord for a Halloween mask."

The sun was going down when the agents left the Field Office, and neither Fowler nor Kendall was up for the six-hour drive back to D.C. "I say we find rooms for the night then go in search of a thick, juicy steak."

"Not even in that order," Fowler said. "I think my stomach's digesting itself."

"Sometimes I wonder if this job is making me too callous, to be hungry after what we saw today."

"No, it's just taught us to compartmentalize."

"Five syllables; I'm impressed."

"It's like an off-duty cop going home and taking off his uniform and hanging it in the closet. Done for the day, back to his other life."

"I wonder what Doctor Smith would say about that?"

Fowler thought about it. "What's the fancy word for split personality—schizophrenia."

"Another five-banger. I'm going to have to start reading Webster's Dictionary at night to keep up."

"Right now, the objective is one syllable: food."

The George Wythe Hotel wasn't the Waldorf Astoria, but the rooms were adequate. The hotel restaurant, however, was great. After a meal and a beer Fowler and Kendall called it a night. In his room, Fowler had two calls to make. The first was to Taylor Smith to postpone their appointment. The Sofitel switchboard rang her room but she wasn't in. "I'm sorry, sir, Miss Smith is out at the moment."

"Please give her a message for me. This is Agent Daniel Fowler." He spelled it. "Please tell her I will be unable to make our meeting tomorrow, but I will contact her when I return to D.C."

The operator read back the message, and Fowler hung up. His next call was to Sally. He let the phone ring twelve times and decided to call again in an hour. He switched on the room's cathedral radio and as it warmed up, music faded in, fiddles and banjos, old-time tunes. Fowler slumped into an armchair too tired to bother changing the station and shook a Lucky Strike from the pack. As he lit it, the music stopped, and following a four-note chime an announcer gave the call letters WDBJ, Roanoke and began delivering the ten o'clock news.

"Local and State Police are baffled by the grisly decapitation murders of a Wytheville real estate agent and his secretary whose bodies were discovered in his office this morning. An odd detail: the killer apparently put the heads of the corpses on each other's bodies. The investigation is continuing. In other news …"

Roanoke. Fifty miles away. People would be hearing about it over breakfast in San Francisco. Fowler pondered Taylor Smith's suggestion that there might be more than one killer and dismissed the idea. The precise incisions and stitching were identical, even though other details differed. He finished his cigarette and decided to call Sally again. This time she answered on the third ring.

"Hi, Dan, I just got in. I went out to dinner."

"Should I be jealous?"

"Not remotely. I went with another woman, Taylor Smith. She called me at the office and said she was writing a paper for a conference and wanted to talk about what it was like working in the Bureau—'The Boy's Club' as she put it."

"Did you tell her you got to work alongside the man of your dreams?"

Sally laughed. "Sure, and I told her it wasn't bad working with you either. I told her the Bureau was even-handed with me, but I felt resentment from some of the agents who think I should be home in an apron beating rugs and cooking a pot roast. She said they felt threatened by a woman with a gun, some gobbledygook about taking their penis away."

"Sounds like Doctor Smith."

"She told me about her career. She's had a fight every rung of the ladder. You have to be an M.D. before you can become a psychiatrist, and men routinely thought she was a nurse. She's had no respect from the start. Eight universities have turned her down for faculty positions. They never admitted it overtly, but she's sure it was because she's a woman. She'd apply as Taylor Smith, and it lasted til she showed up for an interview. Lately she's been monitoring the tests of—what was her word? psychotropic?—yeah, psychotropic drugs for some big company. That and consulting with police departments. Did you know she broke the Sutherland case in Minnesota?"

"Refresh my memory."

"Grant Sutherland's family was wealthy, and he wasn't. He wanted his elderly parents' money. His father was dying from cancer, but his mother would probably have lived to a hundred. He stood on their backs and strangled them simultaneously with a rope that had a noose at either end. Then he ransacked the house to make it look like a robbery. The Minneapolis police knew he was guilty as hell, and arrested him, but all they had was circumstantial evidence."

"How did Smith crack the case?"

"She interviewed him on the pretext that she was determining whether he was sane enough to stand trial. She manipulated him into talking about his childhood, and found his mother was a sore spot. He was an only child, and apparently unplanned. When he misbehaved, instead of sitting him in a corner like most parents, his mother put a dog collar on him and chained him to a post in the basement."

"So he got revenge in kind."

"Right. Taylor kept prying at him, making him talk about it, and finally he broke down and said that he killed them. There was a wire recorder hidden under the table taking down every word."

"I get the mother, but why the father if he was dying anyway?"

"That's the kicker; he told Taylor, 'And he let her do it!'"

"I guess that makes her an asset to investigations."

"She's carving out her own niche in the Justice system. She travels a lot, consulting on cases all over the country. But what she really wants is one job in one place."

"And being a woman, she's given second-hand treatment."

"That, and she's not taken seriously. Men look at her as a pretty woman, not as a professional."

"The price you pay for looking like a movie star."

"I guess. So what's happening with your case?"

For the next ten minutes, Dan related the events of the day and the details of the investigation. "The State Police are thorough professionals. They don't need us here. Larry and I will be driving back in the morning."

"At least you aren't chasing somebody who's shooting at you."

"I'm not so sure I like this any better."

"Goodnight, Dan."

The next morning, over breakfast, Fowler and Kendall talked about anything but the case because the hotel dining room was only half empty at six-thirty and they didn't want to spoil anybody's breakfast with overheard details. "There'll be enough time for that on the drive back," Fowler said.

The waitress, a pretty young redhead with the name Cora stitched on her uniform came back to fill their cups three times. "I think she likes me," Kendall said.

"She's probably angling for a bigger tip. Don't leave one, and see how much she likes you then."

As they left the hotel, a stocky little man in shabby clothes got up from the curb and came toward them. He wore a suit coat that was a size too large and didn't match his trousers. The left sleeve was pinned cuff to shoulder with no arm under it. His graying hair hadn't seen a comb recently and hung in greasy hanks over his forehead and his ears. His hands trembled as did his unshaven chin.

"Could you fellows help a veteran out? Old Johnny ain't ate in two days. All he needs is fifty cents for breakfast."

"Sure pal. I'll help you." Larry was digging in his pocket for change when Fowler looked down at the panhandler's feet. He was wearing a shiny new pair of black brogans. On the beggar's feet, the shoes looked not only too new but too long for his feet.

"Look at his shoes, Larry. What size would you say they were?"

"Look like elevens to me."

Fowler reached into his pocket and instead of change, he pulled out his badge. His face melted from a look of compassion to steely menace. "FBI, Johnny. Where'd you get those shoes?"

The beggar' eyes widened and he turned to run, but Kendall caught him by the back of his coat and marched him to a sidewalk bench. The agents bookended him. "One more time, Johnny: where'd you get those shoes?"

" Found 'em," the terrified panhandler squealed. " Didn't steal nothin', honest. Old Johnny found 'em! He found 'em!"

"Where?"

"In the alley."

"What alley?"

"Back of Doctor Murphy's office."

"The dentist. Next to Bennet Real Estate," Kendall said.

"Show us."

Johnny started to cry. "Finders keepers," he sobbed. "Found 'em fair and square. Don't make me give 'em back. Please."

"We'll get you another pair," Fowler said. "Just show us where you found these."

It was a short walk to the alley. Johnny led them to a line of trash cans a few doors down the block from Bennet's office. "Trumbull's team went through all the cans in the alley and didn't find anything useful." Fowler turned to Johnny. "When did you find these shoes?"

"Yesterday. Found them yesterday, early in the morning before the garbage men come through and take all the good stuff."

"Come with us, Johnny," Fowler said.

"Where we going?"

"To the police station."

"Johnny's eyes bulged. "No! No! Don't take Old Johnny to jail!" he whined. "He ain't done nothing wrong."

"Take it easy, Johnny," Kendall said. "You're not in any trouble. Just come with us. We'll see you get something to eat."

In ten minutes, they were sitting in an interrogation room of the Field Office. Johnny untied the laces of one of the brogans with a one-handed dexterity that surprised the agents and took it off. The yellowed nail of his big toe curled through a hole in his sock like a talon. He handed the shoe to Kendall. "You'll give it back to old Johnny won't you?"

Kendall turned the shoe over in his hands. The Florsheim logo was on the heel. He held it by the edges of the sole. "These are clean."

"Old Johnny scrubbed 'em real good top and bottom. They was sticky."

Kendall used his pocket knife to dig between the sole and the welt. "Take a look at this," he said. The knife had dark brown sludge on its tip. "I'd bet a fin that's dried blood."

"I'm sure you're right. It's too bad he washed them. That ruins any chance of prints on the leather."

At that moment, Trumbull came in. "What have we got?"

"Maybe something, maybe nothing." Fowler explained what had happened as Larry continued to examine the shoe.

"Florsheim Strider," Kendall read the markings inside the left shoe. "Stock number S-292." He reached into the shoe and pulled a wad of rags from the toe. "Did you put these in the shoe, Johnny?"

"They was in there when old Johnny found them. They fit me okay, so I left 'em in."

"Looks like you two were right about the killer's feet," Trumbull said, jotting down the information. "We'll check with the stores that sell Florsheims and see whether any of them sold a pair of these in size eleven recently."

"Let's see the other shoe," Fowler said.

"You'll give 'em back?" Johnny eyed Fowler suspiciously.

"We'll do better than that," Fowler said. "We'll find you a pair that fits." He turned to Trumbull, who nodded agreement. Johnny surrendered the other shoe. "Is there any reason we shouldn't take these with us?" Fowler asked Trumbull.

"Go ahead. You boys have the fancy Crime Lab. Maybe they'll turn up something."

Kendall peeled a ten off his roll. "Get him a new pair of shoes and some breakfast then cut him loose."

In the car, Fowler and Kendall kicked around the new development in the case.

"What do you think?" Fowler asked.

"About Old Johnny? I believe him. Imagine him with a Lister knife."

"Liston."

"What?"

"It's Liston knife, not Lister."

Kendall nodded. "Right. And one-handed, Johnny couldn't do the stitching."

"I don't get the shoes. Why dump them so close to the crime scene?"

"Maybe the killer wanted to get rid of them in a hurry, afraid someone would notice the wrong size. I'd imagine they looked like clown feet. Or maybe the killer wanted the police to find them, but Johnny found them first."

"Why would the killer want that?"

"Like I told Sangston," Kendall said around his cigarette, "crazy people do crazy things."

"We'll get these shoes to the lab, and in the meantime, Trumbull will find out whether they may have been bought locally."

"Somebody spared no expense. Florsheims ain't cheap."

"So now we're looking for a small killer with a big bankroll."

"Don't remind me."

The sky had clouded earlier, and then the rain came, pelting the car like bullets.

Lightning lit the car's interior as if the newspaper shutterbugs were out there shooting through the windows. Fowler thought about the reporters. In a sense, their job was a lot like his; they too had to dig and pry to uncover things people wanted to stay buried and bring them into the light.

"I think this rain followed us from Florida," Kendall said.

"Just like Joe Btfsplk."

"Who?"

"You don't read *Li'l Abner* in the funnies? He's the guy who walks around with a rain cloud over his head."

"Oh yeah, the jinx. Well, it can't rain forever."

"One can only hope."

By the time the agents returned to Washington, the rain was done, the sun was out, and the city was steamy. Word had come back from Trumbull: of the two shoe stores in Wytheville that carried Florsheim shoes, neither had recently sold a pair of size eleven Florsheim Striders.

"Well, there goes another lead out the window," Kendall was disgusted.

"It's not a complete dead end. Now we know the killer's not King Kong."

"Unless, of course, he wore the shoes then stuffed rags into the toes before he put them in the trash can to make us think he was smaller."

"Don't complicate things, Larry. Remember Ockham's Razor."

"Yeah, the simplest solution to a problem is probably the correct one."

"And we're going to use Ockham's Razor to cut this freak's throat."

The phone rang. "Fowler."

"It's Taylor." the silky voice said. "Sorry we missed our appointment, Dan. I read the news in the paper this morning. Number four. The killer didn't wait for the New Moon."

"That's something I want to discuss, plus a few other variations."

"Really?"

"I can't talk about it over the phone—protocol. Can you come in now?"

"I'll be there in a half hour." The phone clicked in Fowler's ear and she was gone.

"Stick around, Larry. I want you in on this meeting."

"Wouldn't miss it for the world." He rubbed his chin. "Speaking of razors, maybe I'll go downstairs and shave for the occasion."

Twenty minutes later, Taylor Smith arrived. She wore a pale blue shantung dress with a neckline that showed a little cleavage and dark stockings tucked into patent leather pumps. Her hair was loose today and framed her face like a dark mane.

"Doctor Taylor Smith, this is my partner, Agent Lawrence Kendall. Larry, Doctor Smith."

They shook hands. "Pleased to meet you," she said, holding Larry's hand a heartbeat or two longer than might be ordinary. "Dan didn't tell me he had so handsome a partner."

Larry's smile broadened an inch. "And you don't exactly look like a doctor."

Fowler saw something flicker across her eyes for an instant, then her smile broadened too.

They sat, and Fowler began. "There have been some interesting developments."

Taylor took out her pad and pencil. "Please tell me all about it."

For the next half hour Fowler and Kendall related the details of the crime scene. When Fowler mentioned the footprints, Taylor nodded. "That's brilliant. On the killer's part and yours. *Kudos* to you for seeing it."

"A vagrant found the oversized shoes with rags stuffed in the toes nearby," Larry said. "They are at the crime lab now."

"What are they looking for?"

"Traces of blood, fibers, hair, anything."

"Any chance of fingerprints?"

"No, Old Johnny, the vagrant, scrubbed them clean because as he put it, they were 'sticky.' That pretty much kills any chance of prints on the shiny leather."

"That's too bad," Taylor said.

"Now, tell us," Fowler said, "Why didn't the killer stick to the schedule?"

"I'd say at first glance, the killer's sense of urgency is heightening. Ritual is important to compulsives, but the killer may have been unable to restrain himself."

"But this was no spur of the moment event, was it?" Kendall said. "I don't think the killer was just passing through Wytheville and said to himself, 'I feel like killing somebody. I know, I'll kill a real estate agent.'"

"You're right. This had to have been planned. The after-hours appointment; the killer had to have observed Bennet and his office to know their hours, that they were closed on Wednesday, and that other businesses on the street were closed too."

"The office hours are on the door, including 'Closed Wednesday.'"

"Okay, but this Drew Morgan person made the appointment at what time?"

"Six thirty. The autopsy showed both victims had eaten supper, so they left the office and returned. The killer knew the office would be closed Wednesday but not about the cleaning lady. Otherwise the bodies may not have been discovered til Thursday."

"Six-thirty, allowing time for other businesses to close and the street to clear."

"Right," said Fowler. "I agree this wasn't an impulse killing. He planned the whole thing."

"Any luck on the name?"

"None so far."

"It's interesting that the killer—if Drew Morgan is the killer—used an androgynous name."

"Androgynous?" Kendall said.

"Nondistinguishable as either male or female. It's possible the killer may be a woman."

"We haven't ruled that out," Fowler said. "I say 'he' just as the custom of the English language."

Smith looked around her watch. "I'd better get going. You've given me a lot to think about. We should talk again tomorrow."

"All right," Fowler agreed. "I'll call once I know my schedule."

Taylor rose and Larry rose with her. "I'll walk you out. I'll talk with you later, Dan."

As they left, Fowler chuckled to himself. Larry was making a move, but he might be getting a lot more than he bargained for in a lady psychiatrist.

As usual, he had a stack of memos, reports, and correspondence to wade through. He started with the memos. Four were calls from reporters request-

"That's too bad."

ing an interview Or a callback. Under them, he found a letter. The plain white envelope was addressed on a typewriter: Agent Daniel Fowler, Federal Bureau of Investigation, Washington D.C. The word "PERSONAL" was typed in the lower right hand corner. The postmark dated the letter three days earlier and gave the origin as Wytheville, Virginia.

An alarm bell went off in Fowler's head. He held the envelope in the folds of his handkerchief and used his pocket knife to slit it open. Inside was a single sheet of stationery. Handling it carefully to keep his fingerprints off the paper, he unfolded it.

A single sentence was typewritten on the center of the page:

WHO'S IN CHARGE NOW?

Fowler felt his face flush with anger. He picked up the phone and hoped Kendall hadn't left the building. Yes, suddenly, it was "personal."

"Let me get this straight," Kendall said. "This was postmarked the day before the murders?"

"Yes. At ten thirty-one in the morning. According to Trumbull, Wytheville has its primary Post Office on Main Street and a branch office across town. I'd bet, though, that the killer put it a street box either early in the day on Monday or even Sunday night."

"So the freak was in town at least a day before Bennet and Watts were killed, maybe two, and mailed this to you in advance."

"I'm sure Trumbull's checking the hotels for out-of-towners."

"But remember the match in Bedford, from a restaurant twenty miles away. The killer could have stayed anywhere and popped in to Wytheville to do his dirty work."

"The question is: how did the killer know I'd be on the case?"

"That's a puzzle. Our names made some of the papers because of the incident at the Wytheville morgue, but that was after the fact."

"Maybe Hargrove; he's been nosing around in Bedford. Maybe he dropped our names to give himself some clout—or one of the people from Cape Cod or Akron. Maybe it was in one of the local papers following the case. Maybe the crazy likes to read about himself."

"I suppose that's possible," Fowler said, unconvinced. "So why do I get this and not you?"

"Because you're famous and I'm not. You're Dan Fowler, The Man Who Saved FDR. That buys you all the fan mail."

Fowler rolled his eyes. He wanted to tell Larry that the whole incident was a sham, that the man he saved from abduction wasn't the President, but a lookalike. He was sworn to secrecy by the Director and couldn't even tell Sally the truth.

"I'll send it to the Crime Lab. Maybe the killer got careless and left a stray print on the paper or the envelope, but I'm not holding my breath."

"Yeah. Whoever this guy is, he seems to know how to cover his tracks pretty well."

"He anticipates procedure, knows what steps the investigation would follow."

"Do you think it's a cop?"

"It could be, or worse."

"What could be worse?" Larry put a cigarette in his mouth and flicked his lighter with his thumb.

"One of us."

Larry's hand stopped halfway to the cigarette. "Holy hell. I hadn't even thought of that."

"It makes some sense. We all know procedure, and we travel all over the country. And as tight-lipped as the Bureau wants us to be, people still talk."

Larry lit his cigarette, took a long drag, and blew out the smoke before saying, "And as much as we hate to think about it, the shit we deal with day to day has to have its effect on us. What you said about hanging your uniform in the closet at the end of the day; that only goes so far."

"It's a scary thought. We'll have to run that past Doctor Smith."

"I'll do it. We're having dinner tonight."

"That was fast."

Larry grinned. "*Carpe diem*, buddy. See you in the morning." Larry left whistling.

Fowler looked at his calendar. New Moon in ten days. Would the killer strike again on schedule, or did the Wytheville murders satisfy his bloodlust for the month? Or would he feel the urge sooner?

Dan had never paid much attention to psychology before; his job was good guys and bad guys; robbery, hijacking, bootlegging, counterfeiting. Motives were simple: all for money. Most killings he'd dealt with were crimes of the moment, but not these. He'd never seen such a combination of homicidal mania yoked to cold, fiendishly clever premeditation. *I hate to admit it*, Dan thought, *but Taylor Smith and her theories may be the key to solving the case. Whatever works.*

Time to walk the letter down to the Crime Lab.

The next morning, Larry was in good spirits.

"Looks like your evening went well," Fowler observed.

"You know me." he grinned. "I don't kiss and tell, I don't miss and tell. Keeps 'em guessing. But I will say this, Taylor Smith is a remarkable woman.

She's brilliant."

"I thought your motto was 'the dumber the better.'"

"Not this time. I took her to Armand's, and when we walked in, I could almost see the cartoon balloon over the head of every guy in the place thinking, 'lucky bastard.'"

"Sounds auspicious."

"Any word from the Crime Lab?"

"You were right about the shoes. There was blood under the welt. Nothing else of note. Still waiting for their findings on the letter."

"As careful as the killer's been, I doubt they'll find anything."

"Maybe they will. Something Doctor Smith said yesterday, heightened urgency—maybe it'll make the killer careless."

"We should be so lucky."

Little happened on the case for the next week as procedural wheels slowly turned in four cities, for everyone but the press. The suppressed information about the murders erupted from the newspapers and radio like pus from a lanced boil. Yancey Abrams from the *Washington Post* dubbed the murderer "the Guillotine Killer," and the name caught on. Denied photographs of the cadavers, one enterprising tabloid ran a cartoonish artist's rendering of Bennet and Watts on its front page. The drawing was of the pair side by side, Bennet's grinning head on Watts' torso and vice versa. Inside, the paper ran an editorial accusing law enforcement of violating freedom of the press to conceal their ineptness.

Fowler brought the paper to Kendall's office and he compared the drawing to the crime scene photos. "Not bad," he said. "Looks just like them, Dan, if you know what I mean."

"Probably drawn from photos in the *Wytheville Enterprise* morgue."

"I wonder why they call the old newspaper files the morgue."

"I guess because that's where dead stories go, but unlike the County Morgue, the newspaper morgue doesn't send them on to be buried forever. They ought to call it the 'river' instead; the dead things won't stay down. They keep bobbing to the surface, like floaters we've known."

"When do you leave for Atlanta?"

"Catching the plane at three-thirty." Fowler had to testify in the trial of Bernard, "Barney" Covington, leader of an interstate hijacking ring preying on long-haul truckers. Barney faced four counts of interstate theft and transport.

"I'll hold down the fort while you deliver your expert testimony. Make sure Barney goes away for a good long stretch, so by the time he gets out we'll be retired and won't have to bother with him."

"District Eleven calls Judge Donahue 'Old Ten to Twenty'. I imagine Barney'll get a long vacation, assuming he's found guilty."

"That's where you come in, Dan."

"I'll do my best. I'll check in with you regularly to keep up with the Chop Case."

"Looks like a slowdown for the moment." Kendall paused. "I hate to say it, but til he kills again."

"Don't even think that. Maybe he'll be like Jack the Ripper, meet some self-imposed quota and quit."

"Then we might never know who he is, but whether we stop him or he stops himself, all's well that ends well."

"You sound like the Director. I don't want to spend my declining years like some detectives I know, obsessing over the One That Got Away."

Kendall laughed. "I can just see you now, grey-haired in a rocking chair, staring at a wall covered with photos, maps, memos, and notes."

The phone rang. "Agent Kendall. Yeah, he's here." He held the handset out to Fowler. "It's Dick Haney from the Lab."

"This is Fowler."

"We finished with that letter you brought in. Typed on a Smith-Corona portable machine; the paper and envelope are common. You could buy them in any Woolworth's. No prints on either one, but I steamed off the stamp and it looks like the sender didn't lick the whole thing. I found a partial print in the glue on one corner. Just the very tip of the finger near the nail. I'll photograph it and send it to you right away. I wouldn't call the finger dainty, but it's smaller than mine or yours."

"Do you think it's from a female?"

"It's possible, but there's no definite answer to that question. Current thinking says that higher ridge density might indicate sex, but density varies among ethnic populations. Darwin got us again. One other thing I noticed, Dan, there's what looks like a tiny cut at the very tip of the finger, like maybe he nicked it on a razor blade."

Or a scalpel, thought Fowler.

"Anyway, it looks like a cut that may not even leave a scar, so catch him quick."

"Good work, Dick. I'll be going out of town shortly. Send the print to Agent Kendall, please."

"Will do." Haney hung up. Kendall raised his eyebrows in curiosity.

"Haney found a partial print on the back of the stamp of all places. He'll send a photo of it to you. It confirms that our killer is a small person but doesn't tell us he or she. I hate to leave town now. This could be a break in the case."

"Duty calls."

When he returned to his office, Fowler found a note on his desk to call Doctor Smith. They hadn't spoken in a few days, and Fowler decided he'd better fill her in on their progress, or lack of it. He noticed the number was to a Pennsylvania exchange. Below it was written Room 526. Officially, she was still consulting with the Bureau, but since the investigation had slowed, she was being paid *per diem*.

The switchboard connected him, and an operator answered, "Hotel Columbia. How may I help you?"

"Please connect me with room 526." The phone clicked and buzzed in his ear, and in a moment, Taylor's silky voice answered. "This is Doctor Smith."

"This is Dan Fowler."

"Oh, Dan, good to hear from you."

"Where are you, Taylor?"

"Harrisburg, Pennsylvania. I'm pitching my consulting services to the State Police Commander this afternoon. I wondered if it would be all right to use your name as a reference, you being the famous crime-stopper."

"Sure thing. I'll tell them to hire you before someone else grabs you first."

"Thanks. Anything new on the case?"

"I suppose it's okay to tell you—the letter from the killer. The Crime Lab found a partial print on the back of the stamp in the glue." Fowler heard no response. "Are you still there?"

"Yes. I was jotting that down. You said partial—how partial?"

"Just the end of the fingertip. I haven't seen it yet. They'll send it to Larry when it's photographed and enlarged. I'll be going out of town today."

"Oh, where? Somewhere more exciting than Harrisburg, I hope, although I do enjoy shopping at Pomeroy's."

"If you call Atlanta exciting. I have to testify in a criminal trial. I expect to be back in a few days."

"You catch them all sooner or later, don't you Dan? Like the Mounties, you always get your man."

"Not this trip. Frankly, the decapitation killer has me stumped."

"And the New Moon is coming in a few days."

"Yeah. I hate just sitting and waiting for it all to happen again, and it will."

"Based on what I've observed, I'm afraid you're right. I have to hang up now. Please tell Sally I said hello."

"I will. And Larry?"

Taylor laughed, "He's a charmer. Yes, him too."

They hung up, and Dan rang downstairs for Sally.

"Agent Vane."

"Agent Fowler."

Sally laughed. "You sound so serious."

"Always when I'm hungry. Do you have plans for lunch?"

"I'll finish up what I'm doing and meet you at one. Ernie's okay?"

"Perfect. See you then, see you there."

Ernie's Diner was that combination of location, good food, and low prices that kept the place busy night and day; no *pate de fois gras* or *charlotte russe*, just a good old American menu of steak, potatoes and apple pie. It was more than a diner; it was like a watering hole in the African veldt. Everybody came to Ernie's, janitors and Senators, and everybody in between.

The lunch rush was dying down, and Fowler found an empty booth in a back corner that hadn't been bused yet. Someone had enjoyed chicken and biscuits with pie for dessert. There wasn't enough left for him to figure out which kind it was. The waitress, a thick waisted woman with her hair in a snood and Helen stitched on her uniform like a tattoo set down a cup and saucer and poured him coffee without asking. "I'll get you cleared in a minute."

"No rush," Fowler said.

"Mister, in D.C., everybody's in a rush."

Sally came in a few minutes later. She slid into the booth. "Did you order yet?"

"No, I thought I'd be a gentleman for a change and wait for you."

"You're always a gentleman, Dan. Just some days gentler than others." She picked up a menu and looked it over. "I think I'll have a cheeseburger and French fries."

"Sounds good, but I'm having a Reuben on rye."

Helen scribbled their order on her pad and scurried off to the pass-through behind the counter where she clipped them on the carousel for the kitchen. "It must be a hard life, working like she does, but there really aren't that many opportunities for women in this town. I'm one of the fortunate ones."

"Glad to have you on board, Agent Vane," Fowler said with a playful salute. "By the way, I talked to Doctor Smith this morning. She sends her regards. She's in Harrisburg, Pennsylvania. Ever been there?"

Sally nodded. "Once on a fraud case."

"She said something about shopping at Pomeroy's."

"It's a ritzy department store. I could only afford their bargain basement."

"Working piecemeal, I wonder how she can afford to dress like she does. The Bureau can't pay her that much."

"Taylor's family is wealthy. Her father's some Wall Street big wheel who sold short before the Crash, and her mother comes from Old New York money."

"So they bankroll her career. I guess that explains how she could afford to stay in the Hotel Columbia."

"Apparently. It's a shame, but on her own, she'd have to scrape and scratch. She's brilliant, but her male dominated profession ignores her; the 'Boys' Club', she calls it. She's carved her own niche in spite of it all, but she's frustrated that she isn't recognized by her peers. She's relegated to jobs like consulting with us and monitoring drug tests for pharmaceutical companies."

"That's too bad. She seems capable."

"She's beyond capable. That's the shame of it."

Helen came with a tray, and as so often happens, conversation lagged in the presence of good food.

"That was good," Sally said, patting her mouth with a napkin. She picked up the chromed napkin holder and squinted at her reflection. "I didn't smear my lipstick, did I?"

Fowler chuckled. "No, that's my job. I have to admit, I'm glad I'm not a woman. I can't imagine having to go through the hair and makeup ritual every morning, shaving my legs and having to worry whether the seams in my stockings were straight."

"And I can't imagine having to scrape my face with a razor every morning and tying that silk noose around my neck."

"The Director expects nothing less."

"So, when will you be back from Atlanta?"

"I'm hoping two days at the outside. You never know what can happen at a trial."

Helen laid the check on the table beside Fowler, and he reached for his wallet.

"Put it away. I'll get this one." Sally fished a few bills from her purse. "That's an example of what Taylor complains about. The automatic assumption that you're paying, that you're the man, so you're in charge."

As they walked back to the Justice building, the words of the mocking letter bounced around Fowler's skull like a pinball: Who's in charge now?

Mindful of its current austerity program, the Bureau booked Fowler's room in Atlanta in the Northwood Hotel on Peachtree Street. The hotel was plain brick, two stories, forty rooms, and about as elegant as a dormitory. A product of the Depression economy, the Northwood, originally offices, was converted to apartments when commercial rental suffered after the crash. No matter what happened, people would always need a place to live. Finally, it became a hotel. The Northwood was all function and lacked the style and luxury of the finer lodgings. Fowler appreciated the grandeur of places like the Sullivanesque Georgian Terrace, or the towering Ansley and almost went to one of those two on his own dime.

In the end, he decided that for a night or two, he could tolerate the simpler accommodations, even if he had to walk to the pharmacy next door to buy cigarettes or the cleaners on the other side to have his suit pressed. Atlanta was even steamier than D.C., and despite open windows, the rooms in the Ansley or the Georgian Terrace probably weren't any cooler.

At least the room had a phone. When Fowler called Sally, that evening, she answered immediately. "Hi, Dan, how's Atlanta?"

"Tropical. I just got back from supper."

"Grits and jowls?"

"No, I saw something on the menu called chicken-fried steak and decided to give it a try. Actually, it tasted pretty good."

"I'll take your word for it."

A few more minutes of Bureau gossip and small talk and they said a fond goodnight, leaving Fowler alone with his thoughts. It didn't take long before they drifted to the Chop Case. The Moon would be new in a few days, and he hated being tied up in Atlanta. But if something broke in the case, he could always fly back to headquarters.

In the meantime, the killer had time to plot and plan. He agreed with Taylor Smith that he was poised to strike again, and Fowler felt helpless to stop it. It was an unfortunate truth that capturing a rational criminal was simpler than a crazy one. Motives were straightforward, and behavior was more predictable. The wild card behavior of a lunatic, in this case the choice of victims, made it next to impossible, and the common denominator of the previous murders, the New Moon was no longer a given.

Lunatic, from the Latin word for moon; the word was particularly apropos in this case, or it seemed so when the first three murders were timed to the lunar phases. Taylor Smith's suggestion of heightened urgency offered the scant hope that the killer was sinking deeper into madness and would make that one mistake that would tip his hand. That will surely happen, Fowler thought, but how many more will die before it does?

He undressed, switched off the light, and lay on top of the sheets. Fowler turned his pillow over twice before he finally fell asleep.

Atlanta's Federal Courthouse was a fine example of the postbellum reconstruction that followed Sherman's burning of the city in 1864. It was a magnificent work of columns, red oak, and delicately shaded Georgia marble. The building, like so many, validated the city's seal adopted in 1877, the mythical Phoenix emerging from fire with the word *resurgens*—"rising again"—arching over the bird.

Carl Greenwalt, the Federal Prosecutor was a big voice in a little man who wore a seersucker suit and bow tie. He stood only five-foot-three but his words rolled around the high-ceilinged courtroom like thunder. The case required no legal gymnastics. Barney Covington and his gang hijacked shipments of every kind of goods using a simple M.O.

Fowler sat in the courtroom for most of the day before Greenwalt called him to the witness stand. "So, Agent Fowler," Greenwalt started, "please describe for the Court the findings of your investigation."

"Covington's men would watch for a long-distance trucker, chat him up at a roadside diner to find out where he was going and what he was hauling then run ahead to lie in wait on a desolate stretch of highway with a long uphill grade that would slow the tractor-trailer. The robbers would pull alongside the laboring truck and shoot out a front tire with a shotgun. The disabled tractor trailer would stop and while the crooks held the driver at gunpoint, hook up their own tractor to the trailer, and drive away, leaving the stranded driver. Covington's *modus operandi* avoided kidnapping the driver and running the risk that he could later lead the police to their hideout, in this case, a warehouse in Jacksonville."

Barney was smart enough to not try for an armored car. Instead, he targeted shipments of cigarettes, radios, and other easily fenced items. Barney wasn't smart enough to keep his activity in one state. As soon as he and his people drove a stolen truck from Georgia to Florida, it became an interstate crime and landed on Fowler's desk, bringing Dan and the full force of the Bureau down on the road pirates.

The operation was a simple trap. An agent drove a load, supposedly cases of whiskey South from Macon. Barney's crew waylaid the truck. When they arrived at their warehouse, they opened the trailer to find Fowler with a team of armed agents behind the whiskey.

"And when you and your men announced yourselves to the Defendant and his cohorts—"

Attalee Sturdevant, Barney's lawyer jumped to his feet. "Objection! The word is prejudicial."

Judge Donahue, who may have last smiled in nineteen twenty-seven looked peeved at Defense's objection and equally peeved that Greenwalt had given him cause. "Sustained. Mister Greenwalt, please be watchful of your vocabulary." Then to the stenographer, "Strike that from the record, please." Then to the jurors, "The jury will disregard that comment. Continue."

"Agent Fowler, when you made your presence known to the Defendant and his accomplices—"

"Objection!"

Before the judge could rule, Greenwalt said, "My apologies, Your Honor, I withdraw the question." But Fowler could see on the faces of the jury that the words would not be overlooked.

"Agent Fowler, did you meet resistance in this incident?"

"Yes. Two of Covington's crew drew weapons and fired at us. We returned fire, killing one of them and injuring two others."

"And were any of your people injured?"

"One was shot in his shoulder."

Greenwalt turned to Sturdevant. "Your witness."

Barney Covington's attorney, Attalee Sturdevant was a tall, spare man with a mane of thick white hair who looked as if he should have a mint julep in one hand and a cigar in the other. Fowler realized that his affable manner masked the underlying instincts of a barracuda. He had the habit of fingering the golden fob, a Masonic symbol, on his watch chain.

"Agent Daniel Fowler," he drew out the words as if tasting each as he said them. "You have quite the reputation as a law enforcement officer. Tell me, please, what made you think that my client was involved in any illegal activity?"

"The results of our investigation, that and catching him in the act."

"Let's talk about that, that catching him in the act. How did you decide to pursue this operation in the manner that you did?"

"Victim testimony establishing a pattern on the part of the perpetrator."

"An unknown perpetrator, is that not true?"

"At the time, yes."

"So you mounted what confidence men, con artists, call a 'sting'. Is that not right?"

"Objection! Prejudicial!"

"Sustained."

"I'll withdraw the question. Agent Fowler, prior to his arrest, did you have evidence leading you to my client?"

"No. We operated on evidence from three prior hijackings to establish a *modus operandi*, that is, a method of operation."

"And what if the alleged perpetrators altered their *modus operandi*?" Sturdevant drew out the words in an almost mocking fashion, reminding the jury that they were common folk, unlike this cocky outsider.

"Then we would have pursued our investigation from a fresh perspective."

"So, when you mounted this operation, you were fishing? Dangling bait for anybody who might go after it, like leaving a twenty dollar bill on your nightstand to see whether the housekeeper might snitch it? Anyone could have seized that truck. Is that not correct?"

"Objection! Defense is asking multiple questions."

"Sustained. Mister Sturdevant, one at a time, please."

"Yes, Your Honor. Agent Fowler, I'll ask again, is it not true that anyone could have seized that shipment?"

"That is true, but this specific incident brought us to the defendant's warehouse where we found a variety of contraband in large quantities; liquor, cigarettes, lawn mowers, a shipment of fur coats, all sorts of items, many of them matching thefts included in the indictment."

"When you say 'large quantities,' Agent Fowler, would you please be more specific?"

"How many radios? How many cases of cigarettes?"

Sturdevant smiled broadly. "Yes, if you would please."

"I'd say about a truckload of each." The courtroom erupted in laughter and Donohue gaveled it down.

"Your Honor," Greenwalt said, "this is redundant. A detailed inventory has been entered into evidence and is available for the jury's consideration."

"No further questions, Your Honor." Sturdevant smiled with his mouth, but not his eyes. "But I request that Agent Fowler be subject to recall."

"Granted. You may step down, Agent Fowler," Judge Donahue said. "Please remain available. Mister Greenwalt, do you have anything further?"

"No, Your Honor, the Prosecution rests."

"It is getting late in the day," Donohue said. "Court will recess and will reconvene tomorrow morning at ten o'clock."

Greenwalt waited til he and Fowler were outside on the courthouse steps to

"I'll withdraw the question."

talk. "Attalee is angling for a reduced sentence, maybe a plea deal to dismiss the earlier thefts," Greenwalt explained.

"He looked as if he were trying to make a case for entrapment. That's like saying Bonnie and Clyde became armed robbers because somebody opened a bank."

"Attalee knows entrapment wouldn't fly, but he was planting a seed of doubt in the jurors' minds."

"The evidence speaks for itself."

"Not to worry. Sturdevant knows Barney's going to jail. What's in play now is for how long."

"Speaking of how long, do you think this'll go past tomorrow?"

Greenwalt shook his head. "I doubt it. You should be on the train to D.C. by noon."

Good thing, thought Fowler. There's a murder out there just waiting to happen.

At the Northwood Fowler had two messages waiting, one from Larry and one from Sally. Both said the same thing: Call me. Both gave the Bureau switchboard as the callback number. Fowler decided to call Larry first.

"Agent Kendall."

"It's Dan, Larry."

"How's Atlanta?"

"Five degrees hotter than D.C. Rule of thumb."

"And our friend Barney Covington?"

"Perilously teetering on the fence—no pun intended—between fifteen years and twenty. What's up?"

"You picked the right day to be out of town. The Director called me in this morning. Seems Senator Armitage is gnawing on his ear about his uncle's murder. You know how it works. Armitage gnaws on the Director's ear, the Director gnaws on mine."

"It all flows downhill, buddy."

"Yeah, but whose ear do I gnaw on to pass along the misery?"

"The perils of the profession. I know you didn't call me for sympathy. What's going on?"

"I've been thinking through all this, and I'm starting to think the killer's toying with us."

"We. You and me? The Bureau? The police?"

"All of the above. We see a pattern established, then it goes out the window. We're dealing with somebody who knows investigative procedure, yet clues are left behind that lead us one direction then it's reversed. The footprints and shoe size in Wytheville; the killer dumped the shoes a hundred feet from the crime scene. If you hadn't noticed the Florsheims on the bum, we'd still be looking for a big man. I'm starting to think we were supposed to find them to muddle things even further."

"I'm with you so far, go on."

"The stamp. Was it the killer's print, or was it some postal clerk's, or maybe a secretary in some office somewhere took the stamp off a roll and handed it to the killer?"

"I get it. But the big question is why."

"Crazy people don't need reasons. Or if they do, the whys have nothing to do with logic as we know it, but instead, their own twisted rationale. Taylor's report arrived today. It's full of words I couldn't find in the dictionary, but I got the drift of it. She thinks the killer has some grievance, some axe to grind and the head switching is a symbolic resolution."

"Why do it more than once?"

"Because the grievance is only resolved symbolically. The reality of it is still there."

"And the killer will repeat til it ends."

"You got it, Dan."

"Does she have any theory as to what the head switching symbolizes?"

"If she does, it's not in the report."

"That'll keep me awake half of tonight wondering. Thanks, Larry."

"What are friends for?"

Dan waited a few minutes to call Sally. He didn't want his frustration to affect their conversation. He thought about Taylor Smith and her theory that the killer operated in a unique reality in which black was white and night was day. It suddenly struck him: and man was woman. Put the woman's head on the man's body. Put her in charge.

WHO'S IN CHARGE NOW?

Fowler felt the visceral thrill a bloodhound feels when it suddenly picks up the scent. He grabbed the phone and couldn't raise the operator fast enough. "Operator, I want to place a call to Harrisburg, Pennsylvania, the Hotel Columbia."

The switchboard connected him, and after twelve rings with no response, the Columbia's operator said, "I'm sorry, sir. Doctor Smith is not answering at this time."

"May I leave a message?"

"Certainly, sir."

"Please ask her to call Agent Daniel Fowler, Room 208, Northwood Hotel, Atlanta, Georgia." He rattled off the number. "Tell her she can call no matter the hour."

Fowler hung up and immediately toggled the phone for the switchboard. In a minute, he was connected with the Bureau, and in another, he was connected with Sally.

"Hi, Dan. How's the trial going?"

"Looks like the People will win one for a change. Watching the attorneys is like watching two master swordsmen fight a duel."

"But you know at the end of the day, they walk out of the courtroom, change their clothes, and go play a round of golf together at the Country Club."

"Put the uniform in the closet til tomorrow."

"Huh?"

"Oh, just a conversation Larry and I had about leaving work at work."

"Hard to do sometimes on this job."

"Yeah, when I'm on a case, my mind runs night and day. Something occurred to me about the Chop Case. Let me tell you about it." For the next few minutes, Fowler described his theory about the killer's motive. When he finished, Sally was silent for a moment. "That's heavy duty stuff, Dan. Did you discuss it with Taylor?"

"I tried to call her. She's still in Harrisburg, but she wasn't at her hotel. Did you know she registers as Doctor Smith?"

Sally laughed. "She did the same thing when she made reservations for supper. She said it gets her quicker service and a better table."

"I'll have to try that, reserving a table as Agent Fowler."

"Watch out. They're liable to think you're an agent for Internal Revenue and poison your food."

"Anyway, what do you think about my ideas?"

"Pretty far off center. I resent the male domination at the Bureau sometimes but not enough to chop off somebody's head. Of course, we are dealing with a crazy person. Let me know what Taylor thinks."

In a few minutes they said goodbye and Dan hung up, feeling better than had in weeks.

It was nearly midnight when the phone rang in Fowler's room. The sultry voice at the other end of the line said, "Dan? It's Taylor. I hope I didn't wake you."

"No, it's fine. I'm glad you called."

Her voice got an edge. "Has something happened in the case? Did he kill again?"

"No, nothing like that. Larry would call me immediately, but I'd probably hear it on the radio before he could do that. Now that they know about the case, the news hounds are perched like vultures waiting for the next couple to die."

"I'm sure that doesn't help the investigation. Has anyone come forward with a false confession? That happens sometimes with sensational crimes."

"Not many. I think the decapitation angle put off most of the usual attention seekers. The local police followed up on the few that came in, but they're all dead ends so far."

Taylor laughed. "Pun intended?"

"No. Sorry, I'm getting as bad as Larry."

"It's all right, Dan. Actually, it's healthy. Humor, even dark humor is a release valve."

"You sound like Larry. He told me pretty much the same thing not long ago."

"Larry's pretty well adjusted to his job. I don't think he'll ever resort to suicide or end up in a straitjacket."

"How about me?"

"I think you just need a vacation." She laughed again. "I'll write you a prescription. Anyway, your message said to call at any hour, so it must be important."

"Thinking about the case today, I got an idea as to the killer's motive. Tell me what you think." Fowler laid out his revenge theory while Smith listened without interruption. When he finished, she was silent for a moment then said, "That is a possibility. Actually, that's a fairly astute analysis, based on what evidence we have. Unlike police work which deals strictly with motive, the concrete reason for an action, in psychiatry we differentiate between motive and motivation."

"I'm not sure I follow."

Her tone had shifted. She was no longer the affable Taylor, she was suddenly the very professional Doctor Smith. "It's a fine distinction. Think of it this way: motive relates to a specific action, like any of the individual murders. Motivation is the underlying force that drives the killer to commit each act."

"I get it, sort of."

"If I understand you correctly, you think that perhaps a woman, frustrated by an oppressive patriarchy, a male-dominated society, could be committing these crimes to address the perceived injustice in symbolic terms."

"That was a mouthful. That's why you're the psychiatrist and I'm just a cop."

"Don't say 'just,' Dan. Each of is good in our respective professions. That's what keeps the gears turning."

"Well, what do you think about the theory?"

"I think it's as plausible at this point as any. We have to look at all possibilities. We likely won't know until we catch the subject and I get him on the couch. Maybe not even then. Or we may never catch him and never know."

"That thought haunts me," Fowler said.

"I understand. It's late, and we both need some sleep. Don't worry, Dan. Just do what you do best, and so will we all. Goodnight."

Taylor hung up, and Fowler stared at the handset.

Then for a long time, he stared at the ceiling before he finally fell asleep.

"I wonder why Sturdevant wants me available for recall," Fowler said to Greenwalt. "What do you think he's up to?"

They stood on the courthouse steps, Fowler smoking a Lucky, and Greenwalt smoking a pencil-thin cheroot. Greenwalt blew out a puff of smoke. "That's what he's up to. Blowing smoke. He wants everybody to think he's got some ace up his sleeve. I imagine he was up all night looking for some angle to discredit your testimony. That or he may have just wanted to jerk you around for spite, make you stay in our fair city for a day extra, just because he could."

Two men stepped from behind a pillar, one with a notebook, and one with a camera. "Excuse me," the shorter one, the one with the notebook said. "I'm Burns from the *Constitution*."

Greenwalt raised a hand. "You boys know the rules: no interviews or comments til the verdict is in."

"Oh, we don't want to talk to you." He turned to Dan. "Agent Fowler, do you have any comment about the Bennet-Watts murders? The word is they're related to other cases. Is that true?"

The camera flashed and the photographer hustled to change his plate and his bulb. Fowler took the pad and pencil from the reporter and scrawled a phone number on the blank page. "Call this number and ask for public relations. They'll give you all the information officially available on the case. I can't comment."

"Aw, come on," Burns said, "just tell us what you think. Will there be any more murders?"

"How about a shot of you posing with your gun?" the photographer said.

Fowler shook his head. "No, and no."

The reporters kept up their badgering, and Greenwalt waved to one of the uniformed security guards. "Jake, Get these birds away from us."

The guard, who was Fowler's height and half again his bulk, took one in each hand by the coat. "Let's go, fellas." Over their protests, Billy marched them toward the steps.

"Do you get that a lot?" Greenwalt said.

"Only lately. The Bennet-Watts case has turned into a sideshow. The ghouls from the papers won't let up."

"It sells copy. Besides, you're a hero in your own right; The Man Who Saved FDR."

Fowler shook his head. "If I say I was just doing my job, it sounds like false modesty, but it's true. When you come right down to it, everybody who enforces the law is a hero. They keep society from running into a ditch."

Greenwalt looked at his watch. "We'd better get inside. For Judge Donahue, cleanliness is next to godliness, right after punctuality."

Judge Donahue reconvened the trial on schedule, but Fowler was never recalled. In his closing, Attalee Sturdevant put on a grand performance for the jurors, who returned a guilty verdict on the first ballot.

"It's been a privilege working with you, Dan," Greenwalt said as he shook Fowler's hand.

"Likewise, Carl. I'd better hurry if I'm going to make the one o'clock train."

Fowler flagged a cab in front of the courthouse and had the driver wait while he collected his things at the Northwood. Flying was an option, but the next available flight was at seven-thirty the next morning. He was at Union Station in five minutes, giving him just enough time to buy a newspaper and a pack of Luckies before settling into a Pullman car. Today, it was the *Atlanta Constitution*, and a day-old *New York Times*. Normally he'd read the *Times*, the *Washington Post*, and a regional paper every morning over breakfast, but away from home, you take what you can find.

There wasn't time to call Sally or Larry before he boarded the train, but he figured he could call from one of the stops en route. Nothing to do for the next eight hours but read the newspapers, watch America rush past the window, doze, and think about a moon that was rotating inexorably toward New.

The phone on Sally's desk rang a little after noon. "Sally, it's Taylor."

"Where are you today?"

"Still in Harrisburg, but I'll be back in Washington later today. I thought maybe we could get together for a drink or maybe a bite to eat. I'll call you as soon as I get into town."

"That sounds like fun. Sure, I'm game."

"I'll call your apartment. I have to run now. See you later."

Taylor Smith hung up the phone and immediately toggled the switchboard. She requested the same number. It rang twice before an operator answered. "Federal Bureau of Investigation. How may I direct your call?"

"Agent Lawrence Kendall, please."

There were a few buzzes and clicks, and the phone rang on Larry's desk.

"Agent Kendall."

"Larry, it's Taylor Smith."

"Taylor; to what do I owe the honor?"

"I'm coming back to D.C. later this evening, and if you don't have plans, maybe we can go to dinner—or something."

Larry grinned in spite of himself. "Or something?"

"D.C.'s a big town, Larry. I'm sure we'll have some fun. Give me a number where I can reach you."

Larry rattled off the number of his apartment. "I should be out of the office on time. I'll wait to hear from you."

"Great! I'll look forward to it. 'Bye for now."

Taylor hung up the phone and looked out the window over the rooftops of the city. Behind the dome of the Capitol, the Washington Monument, obscenely phallic, thrust upward into the cloudless sky.

A knock at the door. "Room service."

Taylor opened the door to a uniformed bellhop who wheeled in a cart with lunch under a shining domed cover. "Will there be anything else, Ma'am?"

"No, this will be fine." She tipped him a dollar.

The bellhop smiled and said, "Thank you. Enjoy your lunch, Miss Bolton," bowed, and left.

She raised the cover and eyed the *salmon croûte* in a light lemon-mustard sauce served on a bed of wild rice with a side of asparagus. Taylor had to hand it to the Hamilton. They never served a bad meal.

Time to eat, then a few hours sleep. So much to do tonight.

When the train had a fifteen-minute stop in South Carolina, Fowler stepped off to find a phone booth. Sally was away from her desk, so he left a quick message. Then he called Larry.

"Trial over?"

"Just in time for lunch, but I didn't stick around for that good old southern cooking."

"Just as well. How'd the trial turn out?"

"Barney Covington's on his way to the Thieves' Hotel. They marched him out in bracelets. Any news on the case?"

"The one with a capital C? Nothing much. Some enterprising reporter worked his way backward to the dead teenagers and now they're pestering the Akron Chief for details. I've been going through the crank letter file all morning; the usual pack of loons. There are a few worth keeping on file for future reference, but none that look good for the Chop Case."

"Any of them mention the New Moon?"

"Only two, but a lot of these Dear Abby letters were written before the press picked up on the lunar-lunacy angle."

"I'd better go. The train's about to roll out."

"When will you be back?"

"Tonight. Eight-fifteen, if the train's on schedule."

"Don't jinx yourself. They almost never are. We need that guy from Italy who made the trains run on time. What's his name?"

"Mussolini," Fowler said.

"Yeah, that's the guy. Maybe the next time you talk with FDR, mention it to him."

"Since you can't see me, I'll just tell you. I'm rolling my eyes. Say 'so long', Larry." Fowler hung up and headed for the platform.

Kendall's words were prophetic. Halfway through North Carolina, a northbound freight derailed and Fowler's train was delayed in the middle of ten square miles of farmland while the railroad crews cleaned up the mess. The dining car opened early with apologies from the Conductor for the holdup, and after a lot of juggling and some fancy maneuvering, the train was rerouted and on its way again.

"Any idea when we'll arrive in D.C.?" Fowler said as the Conductor came down the aisle.

"After all this, the best guess I could make is maybe nine-thirty to ten, sir. Apologies for the delay."

Fowler walked to the Club Car. Two highballs later, he settled into his seat, made himself as comfortable as he could, and drifted off to sleep.

Bennie's was busy when Taylor and Sally arrived, but the waiter found them a booth in the back of the room away from the bar and near the tuxedoed lounge lizard at the piano. The after work crowd was already filling the place and soon it would be standing room only at the bar.

The drinks arrived while Sally was in the ladies' room. She came back to the booth to find Taylor halfway through her martini. "Drink up," she said. "I'm way ahead of you."

Sally sipped her Old Fashioned, rolled it around her tongue, and took a heftier belt. "I like this Old Fashioned. The bartender's lighter on the bitters than most."

Taylor raised her glass. "What should we drink to?"

"Oh, I don't know." Sally laughed. "Who needs a reason?"

"How about to professional women? May their numbers increase!"

"I'll drink to that."

The piano player, barely heard over the five o'clock laughter segued into "Someone to Watch Over Me."

Taylor frowned. "I hate that song. It's just another example of a culture that funnels women into secondary, dependent roles. The words to that song." Taylor sang along in a mocking, little girl voice. ". . . 'oh how I need someone to watch over me.'"

"I always thought it was a nice song," Sally said.

"It's a catchy melody, and it gets your attention, draws you in, and the next thing you know, you're singing along."

"Gee," Sally said. "I never thought of it that way."

"It's a little bit more subtle than learning your ABCs to the tune of 'Twinkle Twinkle Little Star' but no less effective. You sing those songs and the lyrics—and their sentiment—ingrain themselves into your subconscious mind. They shape your attitude and ultimately your behavior. Advertisers know it. They use catchy music and mnemonics—"

"Mnemonics?"

"Put simply, memory aids. In most cases devices like rhyme, meter, alliteration, everything a poet would use. Taylor sang, Pepsi Cola hits the spot—'"

"'Twelve full ounces that's a lot." Sally finished.

"'Oh my, it's—' "

"'Eskimo Pie!'"

"It's a short hop from selling soda to manipulating behavior. 'Oh, sweet and lovely—'"

"'Lady be good.'"

"'Don't you be a naughty baby—'"

"'Come to papa do.'"

Sally's eyebrows moved closer together and formed a chevron on her forehead. "That's creepy. I never would have dreamed popular music was a plot to keep men in charge."

"Just like a good Sousa March stirs your patriotic blood no matter how many times you hear it." Taylor waved a dismissive hand. "That's enough of that. We're out for some fun, not one of my lectures. So tell me, read any good books lately?

Sally laughed. "Not since *Tender is the Night.* Who has the time?"

Taylor recited somberly, "'Man may work from sun to sun—'"

They finished the couplet in unison: "'But woman's work is never done,'" and burst into laughter.

"Your glass is empty," Taylor said. She raised a finger for the waiter. "Time for another round."

Halfway through her second Old Fashioned, Sally's laughter came less often, and her words faded to silence. Her expression had become blank. Taylor looked at her watch. Right on time.

"Sally." Taylor said, "Look at me." Sally's head turned slowly to face her. "I think it's time to go, Sally. Stand up." Sally stood slowly, methodically, as if she had to consider every move carefully. Taylor threw a five-dollar bill beside her empty glass and took Sally by the elbow. "Come along." Sally had no will but to follow.

Taylor's car was parked close by. She guided Sally into the front seat of the LaSalle and slid behind the wheel. As she rummaged through Sally's purse for her keys, Taylor found Sally's revolver and badge. She put both in her shoulder bag, figuring they might come in handy sooner or later. She looked at her watch. Six-thirty. Much to do, and timing was everything.

Sally's apartment was in the Northwest quarter of the city, a fifth-floor unit facing a quiet tree-lined street. Taylor was in luck. The foyer was empty and so was the elevator. No one saw her steer the compliant Sally from the car to the elevator to her apartment door. The dose of PT-37 Taylor put in Sally's Old-Fashioned was just enough for her to remain conscious and ambulatory but have no will of her own. Taylor imagined what a man might do with the drug.

She used Sally's key to open the door and led her to the sofa. "Sally, sit down." Sally took a seat on the chenille sofa and sat upright, hands in her lap. To Taylor, her attitude looked like that of a well-trained dog waiting for its next command. Taylor set down her overnight bag and took a look around in the late afternoon sun that streamed through the sheer curtains. Sally's apartment

Her attitude looked like that of a well-trained dog....

was neat and the decor was mundane but tasteful; the furniture used, but well-chosen. Instead of the scandal rags and movie magazines Taylor thought she might find, a copy of George Eliot's *Middlemarch* lay on the coffee table.

Another irony. Mary Ann Evans' classic novel published like all her works under a male pen name for fear it wouldn't be taken seriously. Sally was no empty-headed bottle blonde. She was more than just another woman, but sacrifices had to be made.

Taylor brought two ladder backed chairs from the kitchen dinette and set them beside each other in the middle of the living room floor. From her bag, she took a small zippered case. In it were vials and a hypodermic syringe. Her estimate of Sally's body weight was close enough for an accurate dose of PT-37, and should be fine for the sedative.

"Sally, stand up."

Sally rose to her feet with a mechanical deliberation. Taylor took a skein of clothesline from her bag.

"Sally, take off your clothing."

Sally stared straight ahead as one by one, she undid the buttons of her blouse.

Taylor picked up the phone and dialed a number.

"Hello?"

"Larry? It's Taylor," she said in a light-hearted voice. "I'm at the Hamilton, Room three-fourteen. Come over in half an hour. It'll give me time to freshen up. We can decide where to go from there."

"Sounds great."

"Oh, by the way, did you hear from Dan?"

"Yeah, he'll be back sometime tonight."

"Good. I need to meet with him. Anyway, I'll see you in a little bit."

Taylor hung up the phone. Men were so easy.

Sally stood before her, naked.

"Sally, sit in this chair."

She sat, and Taylor tied her loosely to the chair back, looping the rope criss-crossed around her torso so that she wouldn't fall. Taylor then plunged the hypodermic needle into the muscle of Sally's shoulder at the base of her neck. Sally twitched at the sting. In a moment, her head slowly sagged until her chin lay on her chest.

Taylor slipped out of Sally's apartment and headed for the elevator. Phase one complete.

The reassignment of routes slowed Fowler's train and made a long ride even longer as it stopped to allow the rails to clear. He stepped off in Bainbridge and went in search of an empty phone booth. It seemed that almost everyone on the train had gotten off to call home, or the office, or somebody to warn of their late arrival.

He found an empty booth at the end of a row and slipped inside. He dropped a nickel and dialed the operator, one eye on his watch. Sally's phone rang a dozen times before Dan gave up. He tried Larry's apartment with the same result. He hung up the phone and hurried back to the limbo that was a long train ride. As it pulled out of the station, Fowler saw the last sliver of the waning moon, curling like a shaving from an oaken plank, dangling over the horizon.

Larry stepped off the elevator in the Hamilton whistling "Got a Date with an Angel." He rapped on Taylor's door, and in a moment it opened an inch.

"Oh, hi, Larry. Let me slide off the chain." The door swung inward, and Taylor greeted him in her robe. He stepped into the sitting room of what turned out to be a luxury suite.

"Wow! Pretty ritzy digs. Consulting must pay good money."

"No, there's some kind of convention in town, and this was the only room left. I batted my eyelashes at the manager and he gave me a break on the price."

Larry took Taylor into his arms and kissed her. She gently pushed him away. "Slow down, big boy. I'm hungry for lobster, and I'm still putting on my face. There's scotch and ice on the sideboard. Fix us a drink while I finish up."

Larry picked up the bottle, saw the label, and whistled again: Glenlivet twelve-year single malt. Consulting must pay very well, he thought. He poured the scotch and settled into one of the plush easy chairs to enjoy his drink. He tried conversation, but talking through the bedroom door became increasingly difficult, as if Taylor were slowly drifting away from him.

The scotch was excellent, and she was taking her time, so Larry poured himself another. A few minutes later, Taylor stepped out of the bedroom wearing dark slacks, a black turtle necked shirt and what looked like work shoes. Her hair was pulled back into a bun.

Larry was about to comment on her costume, but for some reason the words wouldn't come. His tongue felt as if it were glued to his teeth. Taylor smiled. "Larry, I know you're carrying a pistol. Give it to me."

Larry felt as if his bones were strung together with rubber bands. Give up his gun? No. Yes. Give up his gun. He took the thirty-two automatic from the holster at his ankle and handed it to her. "Larry, finish your drink. It's a shame to waste a bottle of good scotch, but I couldn't figure an easier way to dose you with PT-37. Larry, stand up. We're going for a ride."

Taylor put on a floppy hat that hid much of her face and a light raincoat that hid much of her figure. She took Larry by the elbow and led him down the corridor to the fire stairs. "Larry, come along." Larry felt as if he were wading through gelatin, but he could do nothing but obey. She led him through the service bay at the back of the hotel and a block down the alley where her La Salle was parked.

In ten minutes, Taylor was unlocking Sally's door with Larry standing obediently beside her. Sally was as Taylor had left her. If Larry noticed that she was naked, he made no comment, and his slack expression remained unchanged.

Taylor uncoiled the rope. "Larry, take off your clothing."

The train pulled into Union Station at nine-thirty. Fowler grabbed a cab, wishing he hadn't left his coupe at the apartment. He'd call Sally and Larry from home. A few more minutes wouldn't matter at this point. Being incommunicado for most of the day both frustrated him and made him uneasy. He wished somebody would invent some Tom Swift gadget he could wear like a wristwatch or carry in his pocket that would keep him in contact with people.

He was glad to be back, not because he missed D.C. or his apartment, but because he hated to leave one case for another, dividing his time and attention. He called Larry first and got no answer. He figured if something broke in the case, Larry would call immediately. As with his earlier call to Sally, the phone rang and rang. Probably out for the evening, Fowler thought. He'd have to try again later.

Fowler hung his suit coat on one chair, and his shoulder rig on another. He was unpacking his suitcase when the phone rang. "Hello?"

"Dan, it's Taylor Smith. Sally's in trouble."

The urgency in her voice startled Dan. "What kind of trouble?"

"I just got back to D.C. a little while ago, and Sally and I were going to grab a bite to eat. She started slurring her speech, and she'd only had half a cocktail. Her pupils were dilated. She had flushed skin and her nose was running. For all the world she looked like she was on heroin. Has she ever had a problem with drugs?"

"What? No! She doesn't use any drugs. Where are you?"

"We're at her place. I didn't want anyone to see her like this. That kind of scandal could cost her career. Can you come over?"

"Right now. Should I call an ambulance?"

"Don't. I'm a doctor. She's in no medical danger now, and if she gets hauled to the emergency room, questions are asked, reports are filed, and word gets around. I thought you'd want to handle his yourself."

"Yes, I'll be there in fifteen minutes."

Traffic was light, and Dan was two minutes early. Instead of waiting for the elevator, Fowler ran up the three flights of stairs to Sally's floor. He knocked on her door, and it swung into a dark living room. The bedroom door was ajar and he could see a thin line of light along its edges.

"Taylor? Sally?" He stepped into the living room. The lights came on as if celebrants were suddenly going to jump out and yell "surprise!" and he saw Sally and Larry tied naked to chairs. The sight startled him just enough to cost him the few seconds before he reached for his pistol and remembered he left it behind.

A blow to the back of his head set off a shower of white sparks behind his eyes. Dan pitched forward to the carpet, unconscious.

Behind him, a figure in black with a kewpie doll face gently closed the apartment door and said, "Do you really think a man could have done that any better?"

Fowler woke to the sting of ammonia in his nostrils. His head snapped back, and he grunted at the flash of pain from the base of his skull. Faint music came through the wall from the apartment next door.

He opened his eyes, and a pale face came into focus. It was pink cheeked and its mouth was painted crimson in an exaggerated Cupid's bow. The eyes were dark hollows. It was a mask, a mask framed with lank white hair.

"Awake? Good. We don't you to miss the *denouement* of our little drama, do we?" The voice behind the mask was sing-song, but familiar. "You have the best seat in the house, *Agent* Fowler."

Fowler instinctively tried to swing at the face, but his arms were bound tight behind him to a dining chair.

Taylor pulled the mask aside. "Ta-da." The wig went next. Her hair was pulled back in a tight bun. Taylor's smile was the same; sultry, enticing, but the look in her almond eyes was glittering madness. "Surprised, Dan?"

Fowler didn't respond. He was testing his bonds. His hands were tied together behind the chair back and his torso was lashed to its front. He moved one ankle and the other. His feet were free. If she got in range, he could kick her; maybe shatter her knee, but then what?

"You can't imagine how gratifying it is for me to see you like this. The great detective, fooled by a lowly woman."

"Sally, Larry, what have you done to them?"

"Nothing much. Yet. Just a little dose of an experimental drug called PT-37, PT for psychotropic. It neutralizes the subject's will. I monitored the testing, and when no one was looking, I copied the formula. It's a derivative of sodium pentothal. Very effective. That and a mild sedative so they didn't come around and disturb the neighbors."

Taylor leaned forward, hands on her knees and looked into Fowler's face. "You can't imagine how pleased I was when you were put on the case; the great Agent Dan Fowler, the ultimate opponent. I decided if I couldn't have C. August Dupin or Sherlock Holmes, you'd have to do."

"This was all a game to you?"

Her expression changed from amusement to anger like switching on a lamp. "Not a game, vindication. I've spent thirty-five years of frustration being told, 'you can't do that because you're a girl.' When I should be on the faculty of a prestigious university or directing the staff of a major clinic, I've had to sell myself like a street corner hooker and cobble together a career in bits and pieces."

"You're not going hungry," Fowler said.

"Because of Daddy's money." Taylor snorted. "I used to send his checks back uncashed, but then I decided to use it as one more tool in the box."

Keep her talking, Fowler thought. "But why the murders?"

"I might as well tell you; in fact I'll enjoy it. You'll appreciate the brilliance of it. I have been ignored my entire career. How do you get attention these days? Want to make the front page? Kill somebody in a particularly spectacular way, and you'll push even FDR below the fold. Get people talking about it from New York to Podunk. The big Who. The big Why."

"And then you step in and supply the answers."

"That's right," she gloated. "Not the Who, just the Why. And I'll get national attention. Then people will have to take me seriously."

Fowler said. "So, this is all a ploy for attention? What does your psychiatry tell you about that?"

"My psyche is far too complex for a layman like you to understand it."

"But why the heads, Taylor? Why did you switch the heads?"

"Isn't the symbolism obvious?" She sneered. "Men are running the show when women should be in charge. Look at Nature. The queen bee rules the hive and the drones all serve her. The same with ants in their nest. In a pride of lions, the females are the hunters."

Fowler could see the flaws in her logic but let her ramble. Her voice was rising in pitch, and her words were coming faster.

"How did you choose your victims?"

"The teenagers were a trial run. That brash aggressive football star; fondling his girlfriend while he was eyeing my cleavage. I learned a lot. The PT-37 worked as I expected; buy teens a Coke, and they're yours. I took them away from Lover's Lane to do the transformation. The first time took a little longer than I expected; learn by doing, but I managed."

"And the Cape Cod socialites?"

"Reggie Albright was a grand example of male privilege. Mabel Carson was just another toy to him, bought, played with, and ultimately to be discarded. They had no idea who I was. Unlike him, I've never made the front page of a newspaper, or even the Society page. He wanted a *menage a trois* and thought I was dazzled enough by his money and his swagger to grant him his fondest wish."

"And the Armitages?"

"The traditional American couple with one exception: Ronald Armitage was the uncle of a Florida Senator. The police kept the transformations a secret. I thought they might to have a detail only the killer knew to weed out any crank confessions. I knew that if I killed someone close to a man in power, he would take some action to call attention to it. The Old Boy network kicked into gear, and you can't imagine how happy I am that you were brought into the case: Agent Daniel Fowler, national hero, front-page news. And then the real contest began. And I got to watch from both ends of the arena."

"So you killed the real estate agent in Wytheville and his secretary then switched their heads to show what? That she should be running the office not him?"

"You're catching on, Dan. But that's not the main reason. I travel so much it was easy to kill people in a wide area, and each crime a little different from the others to keep you guessing. Killing Bennet and his secretary was more a matter of location than professional relationship. Who was born in Wytheville?"

It took a few seconds, but Fowler came up with the answer. "Edith Bolling Wilson."

"Very good. Edith Bolling Wilson, President Woodrow Wilson's second wife and First Lady, the woman people in the know called 'the secret president' because she had such influence through him on national affairs. Some even call her 'the first woman president.' How does the saying go?"

"'Behind every successful man—'"

"There's a woman who gets no credit for her contribution. She should have been the president, not he, but women couldn't even vote yet, and men wouldn't elect a woman."

"And killing all those people will change that?"

"It will wake up the masses. I've got their attention now, and when I diagnose the motivation, they'll get the point, and they'll recognize my genius."

"And you think no one will ever figure it out?"

"They won't because the trail ends here. Larry and Sally will be the last transformation. The 'Chop Case'—what a crude name for so delicately constructed a plot. I prefer 'the Guillotine Killer.'"

"Delicately constructed plot? Don't flatter yourself. You're no Agatha Christie."

"And you're no Hercule Poirot, Agent Fowler. The case will go forever unsolved, except for this murder. The police will find a note in your hand about how the pressures of your job and the frustration of this case were too much for you, and you just had to find out for yourself how it felt to commit the crime." She dangled Sally's revolver in front of his face. "And then you'll put this in your mouth and pull the trigger."

"You are crazy. I'll never do that."

Taylor's smile broadened. "Oh, but you will. I'd guess your body weight at around two-hundred- ten pounds. Six CCs of PT-37 should suffice. Watch and learn."

She cracked another smelling salt ampoule and held it under Larry's nose. His head twitched for a few seconds and his eyes opened. His chin rose from his chest and he looked straight ahead, expressionless.

"Larry," Taylor said. "Bite your lower lip. "

Larry pulled his lip between his teeth.

"Larry. Harder."

Larry obeyed, and grunted with the pain.

"Larry. Gnaw on it."

Larry's teeth sawed side to side. Blood ran down his chin and dripped into the hair on his chest.

"Larry, stop." Taylor turned to Fowler. "When the time comes, you will obey." She set the revolver on the table and reached into her bag. The lamplight gleamed on the wicked blade of a Liston knife. She playfully drew the tip of it across Fowler's forehead and he felt the sting of the cut and the blood running over his eyebrow.

"I would have paired you with Sally, but I wanted you awake and aware to watch, to see firsthand what a woman can do." She paused a moment. "I'll miss Larry. He was good in bed, but sacrifices must be made. Shall I do him first, or Sally?"

"Your plan was clever, Taylor, but like the killer in every detective story, you overlooked one detail."

"Really?" Taylor sneered. "And what is that?"

"The thickness of the walls." Fowler said then shouted, "Larry, shout 'fire' as loud as you can! Keep shouting!"

"Fire! Fire!"

Fowler joined in. "Fire! Fire!"

Taylor shouted, "Larry, stop!" but her voice was drowned out by his shouting and Fowler's. In a minute, a neighbor was pounding on Sally's door. Fowler began rocking his chair back and forth.

Taylor's eyes blazed with fury. "You bastard! Watch your friends die!" She raised the knife to Larry's chin as he continued to shout.

Fowler tipped his chair far enough that his feet were flat on the floor. He straddled the chair seat and charged at Taylor, ducking his head so the horns of the ladder backed chair caught her shoulders between them. He rammed his head into her chest and kept driving her across the room to the window. She crashed through the glass, and if weren't for the chair, Fowler would have followed her. Instead, it caught on the window frame.

Taylor grabbed a handful of the curtains and slashed at Fowler, barely missing his throat. In rapid succession, the curtain rings let go with a pinging sound, and Taylor fell backward with a scream not of fear but of rage to the sidewalk below.

Voices in the hallway. The neighbors had all come to the door to see what was going on.

"Larry, stop." Larry went quiet. "Federal Agent! Call the police!" Fowler shouted. "We have an emergency here! Break down the door!"

Dan's only regret was that he couldn't cover Sally.

Fowler rode in the ambulance with Larry and Sally to Fordham Hospital, and the meat wagon took Taylor Smith to the City Morgue. The Emergency Room doctor stitched the cut on his forehead. "You'll hardly have a scar," he assured him.

"My friends?" Fowler said.

"The man is conscious, the woman not. They both seem to be in good health, but both show signs of being drugged. Don't worry, Agent Fowler. They're in good hands."

"Take me to a phone where I can make a private call."

In the resident's office, Fowler dialed the Bureau's switchboard. Bill Parsons was on the night desk. Fowler identified himself and said, "I need to speak with the Director immediately. Code Jericho."

"Please hold."

The phone buzzed and clicked in his ear for a few minutes as his call was patched through to the Director's home. Fowler imagined him, sitting in the study of his buff brick house smoking his pipe, reading, listening to the radio, or maybe even sleeping, to be jerked out of peaceful repose by the jangling telephone like a hooked trout.

"Agent Fowler?"

"Sir, we have a situation."

Fowler quickly summarized the evening's events. "Agents Kendall and Vane are now in the Emergency Room at Fordham. I have no idea how long the effects of PT-37 will last, and in that compliant state, there is the danger that they may be compromised in some way; divulge information, any number of possibilities."

"I see." The Director was silent for a moment. "Stay with them, and I mean in the same room. I'll handle it."

"Yes, sir." The phone clicked in Fowler's ear. He found Larry and Sally down the hall in a treatment room divided by a curtain. Sally was sleeping peacefully. Her breathing was steady, and her pulse was slow. Larry was sitting up in the bed staring at nothing in particular, a hospital gown draped over his torso.

"Larry, it's Dan."

No response.

"Larry, lie down."

Larry slowly levered backward until his head sank into the pillow. He stared at the ceiling.

My God, thought Fowler, how long would he be like this? And Sally? A chilling thought: what if the effects are permanent?

He went to the other side of the curtain where Sally lay unconscious. Dan took her hand in his. It was limp and cold. "It's Dan. I'm here for you, Sally," he said, and knew in his heart that somewhere in the labyrinth of her mind she heard his voice.

Within half an hour, an ambulance arrived with a carload of agents, and over the protests of the hospital staff, Larry and Sally were taken away.

"Where are we going?" Fowler asked the agent named Strickland who rode in the car with him.

"Saint Elizabeth's."

Saint Elizabeth's, the psychiatric hospital. Fowler understood the necessity for the move, but the thought of Sally and Larry in straitjackets, locked in padded cells horrified him.

"I can't leave them," Fowler said.

"There's nothing you can do for them at the moment," Strickland said, "but if you want to stay, I understand."

And stay he did. Around three, he dozed off in a chair at Sally's bedside. He woke at the sound of her voice. "Dan? Where are we? How did we get here?"

After the fact, all the pieces of the puzzle fit, though the picture they formed was grotesque. What disturbed Fowler the most was the thought that Taylor Smith might have gotten away with it if it hadn't been for pure luck on his part.

It was a full day before Larry recovered his will and his memory, Sally a day longer. Both were thoroughly examined and found unimpaired by the drug. Dan drove them home from Saint Elizabeth's.

"I feel so stupid," Sally said, as they drove away from the hospital.

"Don't," Larry said. "She fooled us all."

"She was a genius," Dan added. "She fooled the Bureau too. Everybody thought she was legitimate."

"She was at some point," Sally said, "then she stepped off the path. One straw too many."

"She belonged in Saint Elizabeth's, not us," Larry added. "Give me a Lucky." Dan handed the pack over the seat. Larry shook one out and lit it. He took two long drags before he spoke. "I'm glad I can enjoy a cigarette again. No smoking in the looney bin."

"At least you two are out of there."

"But we have to go back."

"What? Why?"

"Director's orders," Larry said.

"We have to be examined regularly for the next six months to determine whether we suffer any residual effects from that damned drug," Sally explained. "I suspect His Majesty's more interested in the PT-37 than he is in our welfare."

"Cynical, but probably right."

"I'm starting to wonder if we aren't all crazy too," Sally said. "We just haven't been pushed over the edge yet."

Dan shook his head. "The trouble is that that edge shifts like the line between the sand and the ocean."

Nobody spoke for the rest of the ride.

Fowler had trouble writing his report. He felt as if he lacked the vocabulary to describe what to him was a unique situation. He was used to fists and bullets, bank robbers and kidnappers. Taylor Smith with her subterfuge, her manipulation, was a completely different animal. The best he could do was chronicle events, detail evidence, and hope the Director was satisfied.

The phone rang all day, reporters rabid for comment. The official word was that the killer was apprehended due to "coordination and cooperation among several law enforcement agencies." Speculation and innuendo were rampant once a few of Sally's neighbors blabbed to reporters, and the scandal rags ran with the story, hinting at deviant sex among Federal agents.

But there was no question about Taylor Smith's guilt. The partial print on the stamp matched her index finger down to the cut at its tip. The type on the taunting letter matched a Smith-Corona portable agents found in the trunk of her car. And of course the Liston knife with her fingerprints all over it, clutched in her death-grip as she lay on the sidewalk. So many times, Fowler thought, the evidence shows up afterward, helpful in proof but too late for prevention.

The Director called him in a day later.

"Agent Fowler, Senator Armitage asked me to convey his thanks to you. A favor owed."

"Yes, sir."

"I've read your report. An odd case, this one."

"I've never experienced anything like it, sir."

"We have our Sweeny Todds and Jack the Rippers; Albert Fish for one, but they're rare. Usually they're simply mentally ill. Doctor Smith was a difficult combination of brilliance and evil."

"I'm not sure the word 'evil' applies, sir. She seemed incapable of distinguishing between right and wrong where her motives were concerned."

"I suppose the word that best fits is 'sociopath,' then, eh?"

"Yes, sir. What she wanted was right; what she didn't want was wrong, and no middle ground."

"I am curious. How did you know Agent Kendall would respond to your voice the same as Doctor Smith's?"

"Truth be told, sir, I didn't. I just rolled the dice. I suppose adrenaline affects intuition as much as it does muscles."

"Remarkable. It is too bad that she's dead. She could have provided some insight into the concoction she called PT-37. I'm sure you realize the potential of such a drug and the danger of it falling into the wrong hands. We particularly would like to know who was testing and developing it. So far, no pharmaceutical company or laboratory has admitted to it."

"Frankly, I don't think Taylor Smith would have divulged anything."

"She would if we used PT-37 on her."

To that, Fowler made no response. For one second, he saw the same look as Taylor Smith's flash across the Director's eyes, and it chilled him. The Director went on. "This case has made me consider developing a branch of the Bureau devoted to the psychology of the criminal to apply to cases such as this one."

"With all due respect, sir," Fowler said, "if that should happen, please put someone else in charge."

THE END

ABOUT OUR CREATORS

Writer

FRED ADAMS, JR. is a retired Penn State University English Professor who spends his days writing pulp fiction and his nights working as a singer-songwriter. His Sam Dunne novel *Dead Man's Melody* was nominated as Pulp Novel of the Year in 2017's Pulp Factory Awards, and his Smith Brothers novel *The Eye of Quang-Chi* was nominated for the same award in 2018. His titles include *Hitwolf* 1 and 2, *Six Gun Terrors* vols. 1, 2, and 3, and *C.O. Jones: Mobsters and Monsters, Skinners,* and *The Damned and the Doomed.* His original Sherlock Holmes anthology *The Affair of the Chronic Argonaut* was recently published by Pro Se Press. Forthcoming titles from Airship 27 include *C.O. Jones: Home Front, Six Gun Terrors 4: The Town Killers,* a Sam Dunne Mystery, *Blood is the New Black,* and *Holster Full of Death,* a Dead Sheriff novel. He lives in Mount Pleasant, Pennsylvania in "perpetual terror of boredom."

Visit Fred's website at http://drphreddee.com/author

Interior Illustrations

SAM A. SALAS - has a been an artist since the 70's. His first love has always been comics and comic book art. His greatest aspiration was to become a comic book artist with one of the major companies. In the mid 90's Sam and a small band of friends decided to publish his own comics. Thus was born ZUB COMICS. The company published two titles. One was GREAT GALAXIES! A science fiction anthology featuring all original stories with art by Sam. The other title was TELLURIA a fantasy title. In all, the company published 11 books and folded in the early 2000's.

Since then, Sam has done various freelance projects for local independent publishers including several stories for a book titled WICKED AWESOME TALES, and a few stories for Ron Fortier. Now mostly retired, he is always ready to take on new projects and looks forward to working with his friend Ron on this new book

Cover Illustrator

MICHAEL YOUNGBLOOD-Of Asheville N.C. has a bachelor's degree in art and has done most of his work in architectural illustration and design. He's done various freelance projects since 1991.

Printed in Great Britain
by Amazon

58412104R00084